THE WRITER

By

Sebastian Roberts

Titles with shared characters

Listed in the order in which they should be read

Day 183 - Published in 2015
Flight 885 - Published in 2015
A Trip to Mérida - Published in 2015
Grace: a trilogy; Day 183, Flight 885, and A Trip to Mérida
Weak Point - Published in 2016
Serenity - Published in 2015
Traffic - Coming in 2017
Wisdom - Coming in 2017
Miss Match – Published in 2015
Dragonfly - Published in 2015

The Writer does not share characters with other titles.

The Writer

Copyright © 2015 by Sebastian Roberts. All rights reserved.
Cover Art by Thomas R. Cuba and Keith Locke.
© 2015 by Thomas R. Cuba. All rights reserved.

No part if this publication may be reproduced, stored in a retrieval system
or transmitted in any way by any means, electronic, mechanical,
photocopy, recording, or otherwise without the prior permission of the
author except as provided by USA copyright law.
This novel is a work of fiction. Names, descriptions, entities and incidents
included in the story are products of the author's imagination. Any
resemblance to actual non-historical persons, events, and entities is
entirely coincidental.

With gratitude to Elaine Olden, editor.

Published in print by Thomas R. Cuba
St. Petersburg, Florida
http://tomcuba.net/home.html
Published in the United States of America
ISBN: 978-0-9968372-6-2
2015.10.19

The Writer

CHAPTER ONE

WALLY

Walter Fleegle awoke to the sound of a car alarm. This was not uncommon in his neighborhood. His small third floor efficiency apartment looked out over a parking lot filled with cars, each one with an alarm that seemed to go off randomly. Wally rolled out of bed and pulled up the blinds. In the fourteen years that he had lived there, he had done this a thousand times and only once had he witnessed an actual crime. That time, however, he hadn't seen enough to even be called as a witness. This time, after examining the scene, he deduced that there was a cat burglar in the parking lot. It was a tabby.

Wally dropped the blinds and wondered once again why he even bothered to look. The answer was easy – he had nothing else to do. But he was awake now, and, glancing at the clock, he realized that it was almost time to get up and go to work anyway. He didn't have a great job, but it paid the bills and he was going to earn a decent retirement from it as well. That's the way low level government jobs were: low level, low pay, decent health care and good retirement benefits.

Wally scratched his ass and went into the bathroom for a shower. He hated taking a shower. Not because he hated the shower, but because it meant that he would have to look at himself

The Writer

in the mirror again. If he could have figured out a way to shave without using a mirror, he would've.

Walter Fleegle looked at the man in the mirror with a sadness that had become quite familiar to him. At 41, he was well experienced in the art of failure. Perhaps it was his skinny build, or the fact that one of his legs was a half-inch shorter than the other, or that his features didn't quite sit right on his face, that predisposed him to his burden of low self-esteem. Walter was short too. He was only a little over 5'5" tall, and that, combined with his skinny build, resulted in what he liked to call his 135 pounds of insignificance. He often wondered if his low self-esteem had led to his failures or if his failures had led to his low self-esteem. He wondered, but he also knew that it didn't really matter. Either way, he would never rise above his appointed station in life.

Like most mornings, Wally had to talk himself through this phase of getting his day started just so that he could get dressed. Once he was out of the apartment and on his way to work, things usually got better. His only worry was that one day he just wouldn't bother. Today, however, was not going to be that day. Today he put on his trousers and a flowery Florida shirt and headed to his job. He did take comfort in that shirt. The logo on the pocket gave him security, if not substantive wealth. He mouthed the words and he ran his finger over it: 'Florida Department of Transportation: Toll Booth Attendant.'

Wally hadn't always been a toll booth attendant. But he had always been a failure. Walter Fleegle grew up as the odd-looking kid in a small school in a small town in southern Indiana. The other kids teased him mercilessly. Maybe it was there that his self-image problems began. It didn't really matter. For a brief period, he thought he was going to be able to rise above his social and physical

The Writer

limitations. He had been awarded a compassionate scholarship to college where he studied English. He had wanted to be a poet. More than one of his professors had even comforted and encouraged him by saying that his physical condition would serve to enhance his poetry. Poetry, they told him, came best from a wounded soul. After twenty years, he had found the answer to their encouragement: bullshit.

Even so, his college years had been his best. Most of the people there tended to be more sensitive to his feelings and, if not, they were more adept at hiding the repulsion they felt. In college, being an aspiring poet and being just on the normal side of being deformed, Wally had managed to find the pleasure of women. Yes, women. More than one had taken Wally home with her but none had taken him home twice. Maybe, he had thought, they were experimenting with having intercourse with ugly people in order to see if their other partners seemed better afterward. His mind made up all kinds of reasons for why a woman would have him the first time and why she never wanted him a second time. There was only one time though that he was sure. Tiffany had as much as told him that she was offering herself to him out of pity. She was going to be a social worker and she thought everyone needed sex once in a while. He didn't argue. He accepted his pity piece and went home. After college, there were no more relationships, no more women, and no job prospects. English wasn't exactly the kind of degree that guaranteed a six figure income. Hell, it barely got him into five figures.

This was the state of mind in which Wally found himself as he rode his Vespa scooter out of the parking lot, down the street, and into the employee parking area of the toll booth where he worked. This was Wally's normal morning routine. He was quite accustomed

The Writer

to it and pangs of regret were both rare and easily put aside. Wally parked his scooter and took his place in the toll booth.

His supervisor had turned out to be a nice guy. At least that part of his life was good. Jack had gone out on his own and found Wally a stool that was a little higher than most of the others. That way Wally could be more comfortable working the register. Jack was a good man. Just after Wally took his seat, Jack came out of the office and over to Wally's booth. At first, Wally thought he must have done something wrong, but Jack surprised him.

"Here," Jack said, offering Wally a package. "I won this at the Little League awards dinner." Jack was a coach, of course. "I've got no use for it, but I thought you might like it." Wally took the package and set it aside. He would open it on his break. That's the kind of man Wally was.

"Thanks, Jack." Wally smiled. "I really appreciate it."

Then Wally went to work collecting tolls. When he first started as a toll booth attendant, the things he saw had shocked him. After 18 years, however, the sights and sounds of the passing motorists were no longer as stimulating. Still, he could not help but wonder what some people were thinking when they came through a lane at the toll booth. These thoughts and memories were triggered on this particular morning by a young mother who drove up while breast feeding. She casually handed Wally a five dollar bill, took the change and asked for a receipt.

"You know you can get in trouble for that," Wally said as he printed the ticket.

"You sexist pervert!" she scolded him. "What I'm doing is perfectly natural! You should ashamed of yourself!"

The Writer

"I was referring to the state law that requires that infants under 40 pounds are to be in a car seat," he said calmly as the infant lost its hold on her nipple and white foamy liquid ran down her breast. "Do you know what would happen if your airbag went off while you were doing that?"

The woman snatched the receipt and drove off without another word. Wally expected a complaint, but it never did come. The incident, though, did remind him of the number of times that women had come through the toll lane attired in a much too revealing manner. From his vantage point, he could look down the shirt of most women. He tried not to, but sometimes when the blouse was undone by one too many buttons or when a bra was missing, it was hard to avert his eyes. The girls in bikinis on their way to or from the beach were hard to ignore too. The ones that really drove him nuts were the girls who never seemed to be able to pull their skirt down past their underwear. On more than one occasion, there had even been a girl without underwear.

These thoughts were still going through his mind when his break time rolled around. Maybe, he thought, he was actually becoming a pervert. He shouldn't let these memories come to the surface so often and he certainly shouldn't let them stay there. He was even more troubled by the memories of the men who had driven through in an inappropriate condition. There was no telling what they had been up to and he didn't want to speculate. Wally smiled. Speculating on what the woman with no underwear was doing was much more enjoyable. Wally shook his head. It was time to take his break. Maybe the break would break him out of these thoughts too.

Wally took his package and went inside to get a cup of coffee. The small building was big enough for the supervisor's office, a

The Writer

coffee machine, a snack machine and one table. Wally got his coffee and sat down to open his package. He could see Jack watching him through his window. Jack knew that Wally would not interrupt his work and open the package early. Wally knew that Jack knew. So why had Jack taken it out to the booth? Wally figured that he was testing him.

Pulling the brown paper off of the package, Wally was shocked by what he saw. When he finally got the thing unwrapped, he realized that he had not thanked Jack enough. Jack had won a brand new tablet style computer and had given it to Wally.

Wally looked up to see Jack in his office smiling like the Cheshire Cat. He smiled back, and waved the tablet at Jack indicating that he was very happy to have it. For the next ten minutes, Wally played with it, learning to turn it on, figuring out how to connect to the internet, and finding the programs that he might want to use. It was the word processing program that he settled on as the first one to explore. *Once an English major...* he told himself ... *always an English major.*

Jack poked his head out of the office. "I hope you like it!" he said. "And listen! I know that we have times when no one comes through this toll station for up to ten minutes, so you go ahead and take that out there with you. It'll keep you from falling asleep."

Wally did as he was told and took the tablet to the booth. After the morning rush hour, he realized that Jack was right; he had some time to kill. Powering up the tablet, Wally recorded the incident with the morning breast-feeder. He told himself that he was writing it down to protect himself from any complaints. He was unable to think of an excuse for the detailed description of the

The Writer

breasts on the college student in yoga pants who had come through a little bit later.

Later on that night, he decided that he didn't need an excuse for either of them. Somehow, that tablet had reawakened his desire to put his emotions into words. Somehow, that tablet had Walter Fleegle once again looking at the possibility of painting pictures with words. Somehow, Walter Fleegle could be a normal if he lived in the tablet. Walter Fleegle was going to write.

Walter Fleegle, Author.

Walter Fleegle, Poet.

Walter Fleegle, Novelist.

Wally typed the words and erased them thinking, *what a dumb name for a writer*. Maybe the first character he should create should be Walter Fleegle's alter ego. He agreed with himself and started to think about what might be a better name to use. Derek? No, he reasoned. That's been done and redone. Wally typed and erased and typed and erased. Finally he settled on a combination of names from his past: Kelly Blanton. That sounded like a writer's name. Kelly was his grandmother's maiden name. Blanton was a distant relative. Blanton Winship, a former governor of Puerto Rico, was somehow related to his father. The Governor had been forcibly removed from office by the President of the United States, but that didn't matter to Wally. Kelly Blanton was a much better name to write under than Walter Fleegle.

Kelly Blanton, Writer. Wally settled on the name. Now he had to build a person to go with it. Once again, he started arguing with himself. Why did he need a new person? Wasn't the new name good enough? No. He told himself that in order to conquer his failures he needed a new self-image. He needed one that would

The Writer

allow him to have the confidence he needed to write and publish his work. Only Kelly could do this. Walter was incapable.

With that argument settled, Wally connected his tablet to the second hand printer he had purchased, and started typing.

The Writer

CHAPTER TWO

WORKING TITLE

Wally needed a working title. What was he to do? Did you give the book a title first? Did you give the book a title after writing the story? What if the title you gave it at first just didn't fit the story once it was done? Wally struggled with this seemingly inane question for two days before he found himself at the public library. Maybe the librarian could help. It only made sense to Wally that a writer would get advice from a book. It was there that he found a tattered guide to writing. On the second page, he found his answer: 'Give your book a working title. This gives your work an identity but it also conveys that the status of the title is tentative. When finished, if the book and title match – keep it.'

He wanted to steal it. He was going to steal it. Inside the front cover he found the little piece of paper where the librarian would put her stamp when it was checked out and back in. Wally put the book back on the shelf. It had not been checked out in 18 months. It would be here when he came back.

Death in a Dirigible - by Walter Fleegle

Wally wrote his first working title. Trying to remember his courses in creative writing, he decided that he needed a summary and an outline.

The Writer

Summary: Death in a Dirigible is the story of a party of 103 revelers who have chartered a dirigible for a wedding in 1910. There would be drinking and carousing, dancing and surreptitious lovemaking between a groomsman and a bridesmaid. A storm would arise, crippling the dirigible with a lightning strike to one of its engines and putting it at the mercy of the winds. The lightning also had opened a small tear in the outer hull of the inflatable craft and it was slowly sinking towards the earth. Unfortunately, the planned route for the party had taken the airship over very rough terrain. The land below was mountainous and snow covered. Just ahead was a ridge and if the captain could ease the ship past the mountains, they would be over a valley. The air would be warmer. The storm would be gone and they could all survive. If they crashed into the snowy peaks, surely everyone would die. The captain ordered that everything should be thrown over the side. But it was no use. The airship was still too heavy. Finally, the men on board realized that the only way to save the women and the few children was to leap from the dirigible, lightening it even more. The bravest argued that they would survive if they fell into a snow drift. One by one, the men donned their overcoats, some even taking fur coats from the ladies for whom they sacrificed themselves, and leapt into the snow. The airship was so close to the ground that people on board could see

The Writer

that some of the men had survived. This encouraged other men to jump as well. The tactic worked and slowly the airship rose back into the sky, cleared the mountains and disappeared into the valley where it landed safely. Rescue efforts were mounted immediately, but only a handful of the men were ever found.

Wally read this over twice.

Maybe it will look better if I print it out, he reasoned, and pressed a few buttons.

Wally stared at the sheet of paper in his hands and shook his head. "It's the fucking Titanic all over again."

He ripped up the paper and deleted the text from his tablet.

He would start over.

The Caves of St. Martin - by Walter Fleegle

Wally typed the words for no other reason than that they had popped into his head.

I don't know shit about caves, he said to himself, *and I don't even know where St. Martin is.* Wally deleted the line.

He would start over.

The Writer

<u>Baseball - by Walter Fleegle</u>

<u>Summary:</u> Baseball is the story of how a group of 18 teenagers from Poughkeepsie learn about life, love, sex, and pain. During their senior year in high school, nine girls and nine boys have a problem. They all took Human Anatomy as their senior elective and the course had turned out to be harder than they had thought it would be. So they formed a study group. It wasn't working. Somehow they had to make it more interesting or more rewarding. It was too late to drop the class and still have enough credits to graduate. Nate came up with the answer. They would make a game of it. They had the flash cards already, but giving the clues and coming up with the answers wasn't challenging or fun enough. One night, before they started the study group, Benson was bragging about how he got to second base with Julie Ann. That's when Nate had the idea. Nate suggested that they put two popular games together. Spin the bottle and Benson's version of baseball. One of the girls would spin the bottle and a boy would be selected. She would ask a question, and if he got it right, he would get a kiss. If he got it wrong, he was out. Then it would be a boy's turn. He would do the same. If the girl got it right, she could exercise her right to run the bases. Some of the girls thought that would be too easy, so they added a new rule. The girl (or boy) trying to answer the questions from the flash cards would need to go by baseball rules. One right answer

The Writer

was still a hit and would still earn the player a kiss.
But to get to second base, the player would have to get
two right answers in a row without striking out.
Striking out was redefined as one strike, so to get to
second base, the player needed to get two answers in a
row, and so on. The game worked but three of the
nine girls ended up pregnant.

Wally hit the print button and got a beer. Looking over his handiwork, he chugged the beer, tore up the paper, and hit the delete button.

One more try, Wally told himself.

There's a Dinosaur in My Attic - by Walter Fleegle

Wally looked at the title.

Putting the tablet down gently, he went to the refrigerator and opened another beer.

Delete.

Once more.

Sand in My Eyes - by Walter Fleegle

Summary: Private First Class Montgomery was
burying himself in the sand on the side of a hill above
an enemy command post in the mountains of Iraq. He

The Writer

didn't even know he was doing it, but out of necessity he had developed the same technique that a sand lizard or a flounder uses to hide under a thin veneer of sand. After a few minutes, all that was visible was his BDU Boonie hat and his binoculars. His job was to watch the command post and report back to headquarters if he saw one of the high priority targets. He was dedicated. He stayed like that for two whole days. Beneath him in the sand he had buried a four-gallon camel pack of fresh water. When preparing his hide, he had positioned a flexible tube through which he could drink. He hadn't eaten the day before he took his position in order to reduce his need for defecation, and he just peed where he was, the urine quickly soaking into the sand beneath him. Finally, the target arrived. Or so he thought. Just before dusk, a small sandstorm had arisen and the air was blurry with the blowing grit. The vehicle pulled up to the front of the command post and PFC Montgomery glassed it with his binoculars. The blowing sand made the image a little blurry, but he was sure that he saw the man he was looking for. A soldier can tell that a man is an officer by the way he walks. Still, he was unsure. Finally, he saw the glint of insignia on the collar and knew that his target had arrived. Moving slowly, he got his radio and keyed the mic. "Charlie Tango. This is Foxtrot Uniform. I have the target in sight. Send in the air strike."

The Writer

Private First Class Montgomery had just called in
an airstrike on his own commanding officer.
Unknown to Montgomery, the target had been
captured elsewhere and the men in the command post
had surrendered. He would later claim that he had
sand in his eyes.

Wally looked at the screen of the tablet. This one he didn't
even bother to print out. Delete.

"Fuck!" he screamed. "How do people do this?"

Back at the library the next day, he continued reading through
the writer's guide. This time, he had brought his tablet with him.
The guide said to pick out an object. It could be any object. The
guide called it a prompt. Then, he was supposed to write a
paragraph about that object. If he was lucky, the paragraph would
turn into a chapter and the chapter would turn into a book. If he
wasn't lucky, he would at least have completed an exercise in
creativity.

Two hours later, he had written and deleted short paragraphs
on twenty-three insignificant items that he had found in the library.

Wally went home and went to bed.

CHAPTER THREE

WRITE ABOUT WHAT YOU KNOW ABOUT

The next day, Walter Fleegle sat in his toll booth feeling dejected. His tablet sat on the counter next to him, but he already knew that he had failed. Once again, he had failed. On a whim, he picked up the tablet and googled "failure." The magic box displayed the words: "Failure is the whetstone of success ~ T. Leith Rettie, 1884."

I should be pretty damn sharp by now, Wally told himself. The quote wasn't much, but it was enough to keep Wally from succumbing to the mind-numbing draw of the three-hundred and two computer games that had come with the tablet.

He would try again. Almost instantly, when he said those words, he remembered an adage from his college writing class: Write about what you know about. It made sense.

"That'll be seventy-five cents," he said leaning out the window and getting a clear shot of a perfectly formed nipple as he did so. Taking the three quarters that were offered, he regretted the experience. As he handed the receipt to the 63 year old grandmother who was driving, he waved at the kids. "Have a nice day at the beach!"

What do I know about? he asked himself.

The Writer

Tolls and tits, he answered. *Is there a book in that?*

Wally took out his tablet and started a log. He would keep track of the odd things that he saw that day. Hopefully, something would trigger a story. He comforted himself with the thought that if Hollywood could make a hit television series out of the events that occurred around a lifeguard stand on a California beach, he should find at least one story in the cars that passed him by.

A Volkswagen beetle pulled up. The young woman who was driving had a Pekinese on her lap. Wally made a note in his tablet.

> Maybe there is a story about an automobile accident that needs to be told. Does the dog cause the crash or save the woman by fetching help?

Next entry.

> A very irritable man, with five children who are all under the age of nine and who are all arguing at the top of their lungs, drives through. Maybe there is a story of a mass murderer? Or maybe there's a story of a father with the patience of Job who slowly turns the Wild Bunch into the Brady Bunch.

Next entry.

> A young man in a Coast Guard uniform pulls through. Is he on his way to his new duty station? Will he be a helicopter pilot or a rescue swimmer?

The Writer

> Maybe he's a mechanic? Maybe he's a drug smuggler
> using the rescue boat that he drives to bring in drugs
> from a mother ship offshore.

By the time Wally got home that night, he had quite a list. Retrieving a beer and a frozen dinner, he sat in what he liked to call his 'understuffed' chair and reviewed what he had seen. He wasn't really getting anywhere until two things happened at the same time. The first thing that happened was that he gave up. There was nothing in the list. The second thing that happened was that he accidentally deleted two entries. Cursing while trying to remember how to undelete something, the words on the tablet merged. The deleted entries had put two other entries together, one after the other.

The first entry was about a cute blonde girl who was apparently on her way to the beach. She wore a royal blue bikini, sunglasses and a ball cap. Nothing special there, Wally told himself. But the next entry was about a handsome young man, who was apparently also on the way to the beach. He was wearing board shorts and no shirt. It was apparent that he spent a good deal of time in the gym.

Wally had something to work with: a pretty girl and a handsome man without two pounds of clothing between the two of them. All he had to do was to bring them together. Wally started a summary.

> Summary: Brandon had watched the blonde in
> the car ahead of him for the last half mile before they
> reached the toll booth. He noticed that she seemed to

The Writer

spend a good deal of time looking in her rearview mirror.

Wally stopped.

"Write about what I know about," he muttered. "I know about the toll booth. I've never picked up a woman on the highway."

Dejected, Wally turned off the tablet, brushed his teeth, and went to bed.

The Writer

CHAPTER FOUR

IDENTITY

As usual, Wally was awake before he needed to be. There was no car siren this time. It was a cat. The little Romeo was screeching like a banshee. Apparently it was mating season among the local felines. Wally resigned himself to his fate and rolled out of bed. Forty-five minutes later he coasted to a stop in his designated parking space, dropped the kickstand on his scooter, and walked into the office. He just had time to get a cup of coffee before his shift started. On the way in, he reflected on his attempt at changing careers. If successful, he told himself, he was going to sell the scooter and get a real bike: maybe a Ducati, or a Triumph.

As usual, the day was going as usual, repeating itself day after day. Life in a toll booth really isn't very exciting. Last year there was a spurt of goodwill and everyone was paying the toll for the car behind them, but the spirit had faded and things had returned to normal. An exciting moment was usually the result of someone who forgot their cash and had no other means to pay the toll. The FDOT, in its wisdom, had developed a form for this. The motorist had to fill it out and then was allowed to pass. They would be billed. The people who had to wait for Wally to complete the paperwork were usually pissed. Some tried to hide it, politely asking what caused the holdup. Wally was usually able to deflect their anger onto the idiot motorist who failed to bring change.

The Writer

But the toll booth is also a place where ideas can come to the surface. There's nothing else to do, so thinking can become somewhat random. Random thoughts were running through Wally's head at a mile a minute. Some were good. Some were stupid. The problem was that a good thought could be replaced by a stupid one before he could get the good one written down.

Wally resorted to using his tablet like a notepad or a ledger again.

About three hours into the shift, a nice looking middle-aged woman driving a Cadillac passed through the toll lane at his booth. Right behind her was a cowboy-looking guy in a pickup truck. Wally made his entries into his log. He finished just before he heard the squeal of tires on asphalt.

Wally snapped his head around just in time to see the Cadillac veer off the side of the road. The left front tire had been shredded and was spewing chunks of tire as the woman tried to maintain control. Behind her the man in the pickup truck had slammed on his brakes to avoid running into her. Wally watched as the Cadillac stopped and the woman got out. She was very clearly shaken and probably felt that she had just cheated death himself. The cowboy pulled off the road behind her and without a word set himself to changing her tire.

Wally's mind started to put things together. Here was a way for two people to meet on the highway and it didn't involve bikinis and board shorts. Wally was quite familiar with highway accidents. Over the years he had witnessed several minor ones. Most of them had been fender benders caused by people who aren't bright enough to merge from the six toll lanes back into two travel lanes even though they have a mile to do it. Some were because there

The Writer

were drivers who viewed the toll booth as the equivalent of a pit stop at the races. If they could get through and pay the toll fast, then floor it, they could get ahead of several other drivers. Wally shook his head as he wondered how we had turned from a nation of civility into a nation of people who wanted to get ahead – even if it meant only by a car length.

Once again, though, what stuck in Wally's mind was that two seemingly unrelated events – two cars going through the lane at his toll booth could become one event. Several events could become one story. Wally glanced at his tablet. Maybe all he would need to do would be to rearrange the notes on his tablet like some giant jigsaw puzzle of words.

After work, with a beer and an easy-bake pot pie, Wally settled in for what he hoped would be a creative evening.

Picking up the tablet, Wally started again.

The Toll - by Walter Fleegle

In this story, Wally decided to take his note about the man with the five unruly kids in the minivan and merge it with the note of the two young kids on their way to the beach.

Summary: Brandon had watched the blonde girl in the car ahead of him for the last half mile before they reached the toll booth. He noticed that she seemed to spend a good deal of time looking in her rear view mirror. Brandon then follows the girl and

The Writer

realizes that they are going to the same beach. The
girl – whom Wally names Gail – meets Brandon at the
beach asked why he's following her. He tells her
mushy stuff, claiming that she's the most amazing
woman he's ever seen and so he had to follow her.
They fall in love. They have five kids. Brandon
becomes the man in the minivan. He ends up taking
the argumentative kids to see grandma alone because
Gail is at a PTA meeting.

Wally stopped typing.

"Shit," he cursed. "There's a lot to work with when they meet,
but after that the story can only go one of two ways. They can be
happy or they can be tragic. They could end up divorced or dead –
or they could end up being reruns of *Father knows best.*"

Wally struggled, but he didn't give up. He stared at the entries
on his tablet, trying to convince himself that he could put these little
notes together and make a story. He had to. If he didn't, he told
himself, he would never be anything more accomplished than a toll
booth attendant. In truth, Wally liked being a toll booth attendant.
He had met all kinds of interesting people – none of whom ever
became a friend. It was like living a life of vignettes. He might have
had other friends, but even though he wasn't in high school any
more, people never seemed to get close. Wally studied the
problem and realized that the story had to be about the journey,
not just the beginning and the end. It was the middle of the story
that was important.

Delete.

The Writer

Wally decided to take the man whom he had named Brandon and the girl named Gail and stick them together with the woman in the Cadillac and the cowboy in the pickup truck.

He started over.

The White Stripe - by Walter Fleegle

Wally had no idea where the working title came from. He just wrote it down. He could change it later. In his story, the white stripe was the one at the side of the highway next to the grass. He'd always wondered why the DOT felt that drivers needed a white stripe by the grass. The stripes marking the lanes made sense, but the one at the edge of the road seemed like a good place to start trimming the budget.

Summary: Brandon had been following the cute blonde in the Volkswagen for almost three miles when they came to the toll booth. Brandon was on the prowl. His rage against women had built up for almost six weeks now and had reached the point where he could no longer stand it. The girl in the VW was his target. There was a short line at the toll booth. Up ahead, Brandon could see a Cadillac and a pickup truck. It wouldn't take long to get through and after that, the highway was empty. Brandon was certain that he could take down his prey within the next few miles. When the Cadillac left the toll booth, the

The Writer

cowboy in the pickup truck tossed some coins into the automatic counter and was gone in a flash.

Apparently Brandon's quarry needed change and she stopped at the booth. Up ahead, the front left tire of the Cadillac exploded in a catastrophic failure. The cowboy slammed on the breaks. The blonde in the VW collected her receipt and pulled out, but to Brandon's dismay, she slowed as she left the booth. The cowboy had stopped to help the woman in the Cadillac. So did the blonde girl. Brandon did the only thing he could. He stopped too. When he gets out, he hears Gail introduce herself to Larue, the cowboy, and Madeleine, the woman in the Cadillac. "I'm a nurse," she announced. "Is anyone hurt?"

Wally stopped, thinking to himself that this was a much better start.

He had put two events together and made the start of a story. No. He corrected himself. He had put four events together and … Wally got excited … he had made something up.

Wally grinned from ear to ear. It had been a long time since he had smiled like that and he rushed to the bathroom to look in the mirror. He wanted to see what he looked like when he was happy. It was a mistake.

Wally's grin was crooked. That only made sense because his face was a little crooked. One ear was a little higher than the other one, making him look a little off-balance. His nose wasn't straight

The Writer

either, but it wasn't quite crooked. His smile went up higher on one side than on the other. As it faded, he wondered how some famous actors could have a crooked smile as an asset while his just made him look like a clown.

Wally was angry now. In a strange way, the twisted reality of Jack's gesture of goodwill that had given Wally both the tablet and the urge to write had come full circle and was now the source of immense pain.

Wally started over.

Death Toll - by Walter Fleegle.

Summary: Brandon had been following the pretty blonde in the Volkswagen for three miles. It had been much too long since he had dominated a woman. It had been too long since he had humiliated a woman. He needed to put women in their place and he would start today with this blonde girl in the Volkswagen. Brandon's plans are derailed when the Cadillac three cars up gets a flat tire and careens off to the side of the road. A pickup truck pulls to the side of the road behind the Cadillac. A man in a cowboy hat gets out to help. Gail, the blonde in the Volkswagen, also pulls over. So does Brandon. He is determined. He is not going to let something like this get in the way of his conquest. Brandon joins the group trying to help the woman, but a moment later, he pulls out his .45 cal. handgun. He shoots the

The Writer

cowboy first. Grabbing the blonde in the blue bikini
by the hair, he points his gun at the other woman.
Momentarily, he considers raping them both. He pulls
the trigger and the woman is spared the humility.
Literally dragging Gail back to his car by the hair, he
sees a gimpy toll booth attendant running towards
him.

Walter Fleegle stopped writing.

He considers what he has written with an air of confusion and awe. Reading it over and over again, he wonders where this story will go. He doesn't know anything about kidnapping women. He certainly doesn't know anything about raping them. He's never fired a handgun so how will he know how to describe it when he tries to write that part into the book? Writing a summary is easy. Writing down all the details might be more difficult. But what made him actually stop was his last line. Was Wally going to be the hero? Was the misshapen gimpy loser of a toll booth attendant going to be the hero? Or was he going to be the third victim of the shooter? These thoughts, while disturbing and somewhat disorienting, had served to break Wally's anger.

Wally was confused.

Wally got a beer and read his last two summaries again. He had written the first one and had been pleased with how the exercise had elicited a spark of creativity. He had actually made something up to add to the events he had taken from his log book. In the second one, he had been angry. In the second summary, his anger had come out in the angry nature of the new story line.

The Writer

Brandon was angry. Brandon was not going to take it anymore. Wally had not described what the 'it' was that Brandon was no longer going to 'take' but that didn't matter; at least not yet. In the second summary, Wally had invented events. The events stemmed from anger. This thought scared Wally. Would he only be able to write well if he was angry? Was his own anger going to be drawn out by this attempt at becoming a writer?

Wally had to admit that he had anger issues. He never understood why God had cursed him from birth with a substandard and abnormal physique. When he was young, he was ridiculed and teased by the other kids in grade school. He admitted that he harbored anger. His teachers in grade school never really did get the other kids in line. The teachers were all women. In high school, things were no better. The teasing was more subtle, but it was still there. Being subtle, it served to be isolating as well. Maybe, Wally thought, that Brandon's anger against women was really his own anger against women. Maybe, he thought, that the way to advance his writing career was to rape someone. That way he could write about what he knows about, like it said in the guide book. Maybe he should shoot someone.

He shook his head and retrieved another beer from the refrigerator.

Flopping back into his understuffed chair, Wally reconsidered. What he had learned was that he actually was able to create events. He had learned that being angry had made that an easier accomplishment. Wally decided to try something different. He decided to try something with music. Wally decided to put on some of his favorite music and put himself in a good mood. The experiment was a huge success at pointing out Wally's history of failure. He was able to put himself in a good mood, but he was

The Writer

completely unable to drag up any emotions that were antithetical to anger. He had no joy. He had no happiness. The best he had ever been able to achieve was simple contentment. In reflection, even his contentment was nothing more than being content with the shitty hand that God had dealt him! Wally was angry again.

Breathe – exhale – inhale – exhale – Wally regained control. This time it wasn't God's fault. This time he had fucked up all on his own. Wally remembered that he had already faced this particular demon. Wally had already decided that Wally was incapable of writing anything worthwhile. Wally had already decided that he needed to create Kelly Blanton. All he had actually done was to create the name. Kelly needed to be real – or at least real enough to break the chains of failure that held Walter Fleegle in his dungeon of ineptitude.

<u>Kelly Blanton - by Walter Fleegle</u>

Wally typed the words into his tablet.

Delete.

<u>Kelly Blanton - by Kelly Blanton</u>

It was time to invent Kelly Blanton. It was time to invent the man that Wally would present to the world as the next great American novelist. Wally wondered what he would look like. After considering height, weight, age, and even gender, Wally decided

The Writer

that it didn't matter as much as other things. The real question was what Kelly's attitude would be towards … everything. What sort of principles did Kelly have? What sort of background would he have?

Wally glanced at the clock. It was late. He would invent Kelly tomorrow.

The Writer

CHAPTER FIVE

KELLY BLANTON

Walter Fleegle woke up to the sound of a barking dog. Apparently the unbridled sex that the cats had been having was starting to irritate the dogs in the area as well as the residents of the apartment complex. Wally rolled out of bed, showered, shaved – while trying not to look at his own face – and scooted off to the toll booth.

In what was becoming part of his daily routine, Wally got his cup of coffee from the office building, went to his booth a few minutes early, and set up the tablet so that it was ready for him to take notes on his day.

He typed: Kelly Blanton: Character description.

Pushing the button on the console that turned the red X over his booth into a green ball, he smiled at the oncoming traffic. Wally had decided that he would put together a character for Kelly in the same way that he had put together Brandon, the highway murderer and rapist. After only three cars he abandoned that idea in favor of using the motorists as the basis for characters in whatever book Kelly Blanton would write.

Throughout the day, Wally assigned traits and personalities to the men and women who passed by his booth. When he started the day he already had Brandon, the blonde nurse in the blue bikini,

31

The Writer

the lady in the Cadillac, and the cowboy. He'd even given them names: Gail, Madeleine, and Larue. He wondered how he would come up with names for all his characters. But a car came through and distracted him.

That was a new thought too and it made him smile. In the past, taking notes on the tablet had been the distraction. Taking notes distracted him from his work. Today, his work was distracting him from his thoughts about his future as a writer.

Paying attention to the drivers of the cars was not really a new experience for Wally. He had always been very polite and respectful. Today was different, though, because today he was looking at each person and inventing things about them in his mind – and on his tablet. A man in a suit was assigned the role of banker. Another man in a suit was assigned the role of assassin. The difference was in nothing more than in the way the two had smiled back at Wally when he handed them their change. Today Wally was paying attention to the actual people.

On his list of things that Kelly would know about would be people. Wally decided that Kelly knew how to read a person's character and intention in the space of a three second "hello."

On his lunch break, Wally went over his list. There was a cop, a doctor, a guy who looked like he worked in construction, several servicemen, and lot of people going to the beach. There were dogs, cats, two birds and one woman with a ferret. Wally imagined a story for each of them.

Wally also started filling in the blanks for Kelly Blanton.

In addition to being able to read people easily, Kelly was an avid reader. He knew about books. He might even own a

The Writer

bookstore. *Hell*, Wally thought, *if I can make up the man, I can makeup stuff he owns.*

Wally wanted to write that Kelly Blanton was an adventurer. He wanted him to be exciting. He wanted Kelly Blanton to be anyone other than Walter Fleegle. But he couldn't. How could Kelly Blanton be a writer who knew about exciting things if neither of them had ever done anything exciting? Wally could wish that his alter ego was more experienced in adventure, but he could no more assign these to Kelly than to any of his characters. No. He told himself. Walter had to do research. If he wanted Kelly to be able to write about flying a small plane over the Andes with a load of cocaine aboard, he needed to know a little more about flying and a little more about cocaine. That kind of research frightened Wally, so he decided to take Kelly with him.

<u>Research.</u>

Walter Fleegle wrote the word in his tablet and went back to his booth to complete his afternoon shift.

The shift ended in the same manner as it had begun. Wally took notes all afternoon as people passed through his lane. For the first time in his life, he was looking at people without wondering how they were looking at him. He no longer cared whether or not they saw him as odd, ugly, or even as repulsive. He was looking at them without defending himself from the looks at him. Later that night he marveled at the transformation. *HE* was looking at *THEM*. This was how he wanted to be from now on. There was a freedom in being the dominant one in a staring contest. There was a freedom in looking *INTO* someone else's eyes and in seeing into someone else's soul that he had never experienced before. In years past, he had always been the one with his eyes averted, hiding his soul, his weakness, his pain, his self-derision from others.

Walter got a beer from the refrigerator and flopped into his understuffed chair to watch a movie. He had the day off tomorrow and had resolved to get a good night's sleep to prepare for it. He read through his notes about the travelers only once. He would let his subconscious work over the data and, in the morning, he would start to work in earnest. The movie was horrible, but it put his mind at ease.

Wally opened his eyes slowly. He thought he must be dreaming. There were no cats calling to potential mates. There were no dogs barking. There were no car alarms.

Maybe I'm dead, he thought.

All he heard was the whir of the motor that kept the refrigerator cold. Glancing at the window, he saw that it was already light outside. It was time to get to work.

Wally rolled out of bed and made a pot of coffee. He was particular about his appearance, or what little he had that was worth being particular about, and dutifully brushed his teeth every day. He showered even though he didn't have to go to work, and then he shaved. He had thought once that growing a beard would help hide his uneven features. After three weeks, he realized that the beard was worse. It wasn't even. There were bare spots and wispy spots intermingled with what looked like clumps of thick growth. And so he shaved every day.

With his coffee and a bagel, he took up his position in his chair and powered up the tablet. Wally needed to do research. Guns,

The Writer

cars, airplanes, and trains, would fill his day. *What was that old line?* He asked himself: *Something about fast cars and faster women.* That was the man that Kelly Blanton would be. He had to be, or else he wouldn't be able to write about what he knew about.

After a while, though, Wally realized that research on the internet would give him a lot of pictures and numerous write-ups about how other people had felt when they went skydiving for the first time, but he was unable to capture the emotion. If he wanted to write about fancy cars, then he had to have a fancy car. If he wanted to write about beautiful women, then he needed a beautiful woman.

It was that simple.

Okay, Wally told himself. *If I'm gonna do this, I might as well do it right.*

For the next ten minutes Walter Fleegle worked his way through every piece of clothing that he had in his closet. He wanted to look the part that he intended to play. He failed. Wally admitted that he was used to that – but he was also tired of it. Wally put on a pair of shorts and a t-shirt and left the apartment. Catching the bus at the corner, he paid seventy-five cents to the driver and took a seat in the back. When he saw the entrance to the mall, got up and pulled the cord to let the driver know that this was his stop.

"Dillard's. Macy's. Penney's." Wally read the marquee. He would visit them all. Walter was going to buy a suit. Kelly Blanton would wear a suit. If Wally wanted to do research to support the Kelly Blanton alter ego, then Wally had to wear a suit. *God!* Wally issued a silent prayer. *Please don't let me become schizophrenic!*

An hour later, Walter Fleegle was in the trash can in the changing room. Kelly Blanton walked out of the mall and hailed a

The Writer

taxi. "Please take me to the nearest car dealership that sells Alpha Romeos."

Wally had no intention of letting Kelly Blanton actually purchase an Alpha Romeo, but he thought that a test drive might give him a hint of the emotion that owning a car like that might bring. Both Wally and Kelly got more than they bargained for.

"Mr. Fleegle," the salesman said. "Your credit score is as close to perfect as any that I've ever seen." Wally had been on pins and needles while the salesman checked his credit. He had been unaware that a person doesn't just walk into a dealership like this and ask for a test drive. The salesman explained the policy to Wally. "If we did that, we'd have teenagers lined up from here all the way down to the donut shop."

Wally processed the statement. Of course his credit score would be good. He'd worked the same job for 18 years. His paycheck was deposited automatically. He didn't own a house or a car. He never went out. The tax preparation company did all his taxes and deposited his refund electronically. Wally realized that he had no idea what his credit score might have been because he really had no idea what his financial situation was. When the salesman explained that he had one credit card and it was always paid immediately for the full amount due, Wally realized that his habit of processing his debit card as a credit card had triggered some computer into thinking that he was a responsible user of credit. The truth was that he bought things that way because it was less expensive for the retailer.

As these thoughts went through his head, he heard himself asking, "So, that means I can go for a test drive?"

The Writer

The salesman smiled. "Yes it does. I've got some paperwork to do so I'm going to ask Lisa to take you out. Is that alright?"

After the salesman had pushed a button on the intercom and asked Lisa if she could take a customer on a test drive, Wally sat and fidgeted. He shared uncomfortable smiles with the salesman. Walter Fleegle had become Kelly Blanton for a little while, but deep inside, Walter was still unsure of himself. The suit had been purchased off the rack and Walter knew that it really didn't fit the way a suit should fit. That wasn't the manufacturer's fault. Walter didn't have a normal body. His special shoe, with the thicker sole, had evened out the length of his legs, but the extra weight tended to make him walk with a little bit of a rocking motion. During the time that he waited for Lisa, the bravado brought out by the new suit and the active interaction with the salesman started to wane. When Lisa came around the corner, Walter had returned.

It didn't take long for Wally to figure out that there was no paperwork to do and that Lisa was just another part of the sales pitch. Lisa was the kind of girl who would have looked strikingly pretty in a pair of overalls. Today, though, as part of her job of closing deals on expensive cars, she was dressed like the models in the television commercials. Lisa was tall and made taller by spike heels. Long, tanned and toned, legs extended up from the expensive shoes and disappeared beneath a tight black mini-skirt right before things would have become illegal. Above that, a form fitting white V-neck polo style shirt provided contrast. The look was capped by a perfectly formed face, with dark eyes, high cheeks, and a straight nose all framed by long and bouncing curls.

"Hi." She smiled. "I'm Lisa. Would you like to go for a ride?"

The Writer

Walter smiled and nodded. In the next two seconds, he somehow forced Walter Fleegle into submission and revived his Kelly Blanton persona. Both of them knew that Lisa was nothing more than a fiscal pry bar and neither one of them cared.

The Alpha Romeo is more than just a machine. It is a work of art. On the city streets it handled well and was responsive to Kelly's every whim. Wally wondered if Lisa was the same, but dismissed the idea immediately. She did this several times a day with men who were much better catches than ...

Kelly told Wally to shut up. He was ruining the ambience of the drive.

Once on the highway, Lisa told him to go ahead and open it up. Putting a hand on his thigh for emphasis, she said, "We'll pay the ticket."

Kelly's foot pressed the accelerator down and even though he had already been traveling at 75 mph, the car leapt forward, pressing them into their seats. Kelly pulled his foot back. He was not used to the speed and he was not used to highway driving. His scooter was unable to travel faster than 55. With her hand still on his thigh, Lisa asked, "What's the matter? Don't you like it?"

Trying to be suave, Kelly glanced at Lisa. The seat belt distracted him momentarily as it crossed from one shoulder to the opposite hip, accenting her assets. As his eyes found the buckle, he also became aware of just how tight and how short her skirt was. He'd seen a lot of women from his perch in the toll booth, some in even more revealing clothing, but none had been more stimulating than Lisa.

The Writer

"The visibility isn't so good," Kelly said, returning his eyes to the road ahead. "The rear quarters are almost invisible and the rearview mirror doesn't let me see what's going on behind me."

She squeezed his thigh slightly. "You're in an Alpha Romeo. If anyone is behind you, they're probably going to stay behind you."

By the time the test ride was over, Kelly Blanton was in complete control.

"I'll think about it," he said." After thanking both Lisa and the salesman, he added, "I need to go see the new Jag."

CHAPTER SIX

MANAGING SCHIZOPHRENIA

Wally had taken a cab back to his apartment where he had been staring at himself in the bathroom mirror for ten minutes. He still wore his suit and had been marveling at how different he looked in it when compared to his Department of Transportation Florida shirt. "How does Spiderman do it?" Wally asked the man in the mirror.

"Every girl's crazy 'bout a sharp-dressed man," Kelly answered.

Walter had to admit that Kelly had a point. In his dark grey suit, ill-fitting as it was, with a stark white shirt and a soft blue tie, Walter's features didn't seem quite so out of place. None of the little oddities could ever have been considered a deformity by anyone other than fifth graders and the posers in high school.

Like an echo that had traveled around the world before coming back, Kelly heard the salesman's voice again: *Your credit score is as close to perfect as any that I've ever seen.*

Walter went to get his tablet and see if he could get onto the internet and check his account at the credit union, but as he powered it up, he remembered that he had never gotten around to setting up his username and password. Glancing at his watch, he decided that he had time to go to the branch office in person.

The Writer

Quickly changing from the suit into jeans and a t-shirt, Wally dashed outside and mounted the scooter. The credit union was only eight blocks away. He would easily get there before closing. Once inside, he knew that they wouldn't throw him out – at least not right away.

Seated in a comfortable side chair, Walter Fleegle watched the young man at the customer service desk enter his information into the computer. "This should give you everything you need, sir," the man said as he hit the print button. Four seconds later, he handed Walter a printout of his balance.

Only one number stood out. It was the one on the bottom line. The number was $120,346.22.

Walter stared at the number for a long time.

"Is there something wrong?" the customer service representative asked.

To Wally, his voice sounded hollow and far away, as if it had come from a man standing at the other end of a long wood-paneled hallway. He heard the question, but his mind was racing. When he had first been hired by the FDOT, he had been forced by their policy to sign up for automatic deposit. At the time, he had checked a box that put 20% of his paycheck into a savings account. After a while, when he realized that his lifestyle would never be expensive enough for him to worry about bouncing checks, he had gotten out of the habit of monitoring his balance. The credit union paid interest on both the savings account and the checking account. The money had just kept accruing. After 18 years he had amassed the six figure balance through nothing more than his uneventful life.

"No," Walter told the man. "Everything seems fine."

The Writer

Back at the apartment, Walter argued with Kelly.

"This is nuts."

"Maybe."

"How can I have this much money?"

"You already know the answer to that."

"I can do things now."

"You always could."

"Sure. Alone! What fun is that?"

"You don't need to be alone anymore."

"Seriously?"

"Sure. Did you see the way that Lisa looked at me?"

"She was looking at me – and she was selling a car."

"Ok. You win on that point."

"What should I do?"

"What do you want to do?"

"I want to write."

"Then write."

"How can I? The writer's guide and my college notes are both very clear; write about what you know about."

"Then know about other things. Isn't that why you went to the dealership?"

"Yes. It is."

"Then it's settled?"

The Writer

"No. I still need to be careful."

"Of course you do – we do."

"I need to work two more years for the FDOT to make sure I get my pension."

"That's fine. That gives me ... us ... time to do things that we can write about later."

"Okay."

"Then it's settled?"

"Yes. It's settled."

"You have tomorrow off. What do you want to do?"

"I'll decide in the morning."

"We'll decide?"

"No." Walter ended the argument. "I'll decide."

CHAPTER SEVEN

KNOWING ABOUT THINGS TO WRITE ABOUT

Wally was up the next morning before the cats. He was up before the dogs. He wasn't really sure if he'd ever actually gone to sleep at all. The night was spent dreaming about the things he could do so that Kelly would have something to write about.

With his coffee in one hand and a bagel in the other, Wally made his way to his understuffed chair. His tablet was already on the table next to it, so once he settled in and put his coffee down, he was ready to get to work. *First things first,* he told himself. He was going to make a list.

What do exciting people do? He asked himself. He typed his answers into the tablet. *They fly. They drive fast cars. They go to fancy dinners. They shoot guns. They probably sail, or have a cabin cruiser. Maybe they are deep sea fishermen or SCUBA divers? Do they hunt for buried treasure? What about ancient artifacts? Wally deleted the last entry. Indiana Jones had cornered that market. He made one more entry. They travel.*

Walter paused for a moment, then typed again: *they probably have lots of sex.*

He looked at his list and decided that while it may not be complete, it was a good start.

The Writer

As an afterthought, he added, *Learn to play poker and some other Las Vegas games.*

Glancing at the clock and then back to his list, he selected something that could be accomplished in one day. It was only 7:30 but some of the things on his list would take planning and even reservations or tickets. He settled on the fancy dinner because it seemed innocuous and innocent enough. When he saw the newspaper, he changed his mind. There in the travel section was an advertisement for a dinner cruise. He could cross two things off of his list at once. He could go out on the bay – which he thought might count for sailing – and he could have a fancy dinner. The cruise was to raise money for the local mission. Wally took more than a few minutes trying to figure out how rich people having a fancy dinner would help feed hungry poor people. *Why don't they just write the mission a check?* He asked himself.

Kelly Blanton burst into his thoughts. "Rich people need their parties to support poor people because if they wrote a check at home, no one would see them do it. On the dinner cruise, all their friends will see them there and know how generous they are. The altruism of their donation would put them in the spotlight."

"Go away," Wally ordered. "I'm busy."

Walter put his tablet away, got cleaned up, and took his scooter to the mall. This time, he would do it right. Three hours later, the tailor and two sales associates had made a very handsome commission on Wally's purchases. The tailor had originally told Wally that the suits wouldn't be ready for two days. The hundred dollar bill that Wally gave him had the desired effect of altering the estimate so that the alterations to one of the suits would be finished in an hour. He would pick up the others after three days.

The Writer

While he waited for the tailor to alter the suit that he wanted to wear that night, he walked over to the barber shop and got a haircut. He'd never gotten anything more specific than "a trim" before. This time, he gave the barber instructions that he wanted his hair to be cut in a way that would make his features look more normal. The barber studied his face for a few minutes and nodded. "I can do something."

He did, too. Walter was very pleased with the new style of cut. It did exactly what he had hoped that it would. He tipped the man generously, vowing to come back every month for the foreseeable future.

After picking up his new clothing, Walter took a taxi home because his scooter was too small to carry everything. *Kelly will plan better than this.* Walter told himself. He dropped his new clothes at the apartment and took the bus back to pick up his scooter.

At home, he called the number in the paper and asked if there was still room for him to attend. He was assured that there was room, but was stumped when the woman on the phone asked, "How many?"

How many? Wally asked himself. Before he could stop him, Kelly Blanton blurted out, "Two."

Walter thanked the woman and hung up.

For the next five minutes, Wally looked through the internet listings for escort services. He knew that most of them might be thinly disguised prostitution centers, but, he reasoned, exciting people probably know about prostitutes too, so the effort would not be wasted.

The Writer

He was about to click the escort services version of the "buy now" button when he realized that every single person on the dinner cruise would see right through the charade. The problem with prostitutes, even internet prostitutes disguised as escorts, was that they still looked like prostitutes. Wally decided that he could find another way, if he really put his mind to it.

Wally was stumped.

Kelly wasn't. "Try singles groups."

It was a surprisingly good idea. Wally had run across some of these groups while looking for local adventure clubs for Kelly to join. There were adventure seekers in abundance, but Wally remembered that there also had been singles clubs, dating clubs, and even religious dating clubs.

It took Wally the rest of the afternoon, but by using the charitable nature of the event and sending a selfie that he took with his tablet, he was able to convince a young woman to accompany him. Cherise was from a Christian group of singles and the charity for the event was one that she already supported. He had offered safeguards too. He would not pick her up. She would meet him at the dock and he would not even ask for her last name unless she offered it.

Later that afternoon, Wally showered, shaved, and spent an inordinate amount of time combing his hair. Earlier, he had washed his new shirt to get the *new* smell out of it. After he had cleaned himself up, he spent ten minutes ironing the shirt. Of course, he had had to go out and buy an iron as well. He was worried about his shoes. They were new and they were actual shoes. He hadn't worn anything except sneakers and sandals for many years.

The Writer

As the hair was combed and the shirt was buttoned Walter could feel himself fade. After putting on his new slacks and adding the tie, he could feel himself changing. By the time he slipped on his jacket and looked at the finished product in the bathroom mirror, he saw Kelly Blanton staring back at him. Walter Fleegle had retired for the evening.

Rather than ride his aging scooter to the dock, Kelly Blanton called for a taxi. It was a short ride, but Kelly was a big tipper. He gave the man an extra $20.00 but made him promise to meet him at the end of the cruise to take him home. He didn't have to wait long for Cherise. She too arrived in a taxi, but looked a little lost when she got out. Without closing the door to the cab, she leaned back inside and asked the driver to wait a few moments. When she turned around again, Kelly Blanton was there to say hello.

He respected her personal space and had not approached to within more than 10 feet. When she turned around, he smiled pleasantly.

"Cherise?"

She smiled at him little uncertainly.

"Hi. I'm Walter Fleegle. I guess I don't look much like my selfie but that's the suit. I really am more comfortable in … well … more comfortable clothes."

Cherise smiled as she recognized the crookedness of Kelly's grin.

"I see that," she said.

Before she could pay the cabbie, Kelly approached, paid the fare, and made the driver the same deal that he had made with his own cabbie.

The Writer

Turning to Cherise, he explained. "He'll make sure you get home okay."

The dinner cruise was a completely fabulous and new experience for Walter. He was very happy that Kelly was there to get him through it. After paying the cab fare, Kelly had taken Cherise's hand by the finger tips and guided her to the slanted walkway that took them aboard the ship. It was small, by cruising standards, but moderately large by dinner cruise standards. At the top of the walk, he had announced his name and that of his guest. The young lady gave them horrible little name tags but at least they weren't the big blocky ones that were used at trade shows. Inside a hostess gave them and two other couples a quick tour of the ship. Kelly had to admit to himself that he and his companion were much more smartly dressed than the other two couples. He also felt that Cherise carried herself in a much more feminine manner than the other women.

The main deck was the dinner deck. The next deck above that was a solid wooden dance floor with a bar at one end and a dance band at the other. The upper deck was open to the stars and dotted with deck chairs and small tables. Of course, there was a bar. Around the edge of the dinner deck were several small tables where the charity had set up a silent auction. If a guest liked an item, he would write a bid and sign his name. At the end of the evening, the winners would be announced, the money would be collected, and the charity would be better off.

The best part of the evening was the time that Kelly and Cherise spent out on that upper deck. The worst part for Kelly was trying to dance. Cherise was very patient with Kelly and walked him slowly through the steps with a smile. The worst part of the evening for Cherise was in the parking lot at the end of the cruise.

The Writer

She had really enjoyed herself and as Kelly was holding the door of the taxi for her, she asked, "Will I see you again?"

"I'm not sure," Wally said. "You see, this is the first time I have been out with a woman in many years and I'm just not sure what to make of it yet. And as I told you earlier, all I really needed was an escort for the cruise. It was wonderful, though. I can assure you of that."

In the cab on the way home, Cherise wondered if he had been in prison or if he was gay. She could not fathom why such a nice man didn't date. Eventually, she smiled. *At least he was honest,* she told herself. That was more than she could say for most of the other men whom she had connected with on the internet.

As soon as Wally got home, he hung up his suit neatly, flopped into his understuffed chair, and tried to capture his emotions in notes that he wrote on his tablet. It was the emotions, not a second date, that Kelly needed if Kelly was going to write.

Cherise had smelled good. The food had smelled good. The rum had smelled good. Cherise had felt good too. When she taught him to dance, she held him at a respectable distance because that was how the dance was done, but after one number, she pulled him close and gave him a hug. Walter had forgotten how nice it was to feel someone else's body pressed to his, even if both of them were still fully clothed. He had looked down enough shirts from his perch in the toll booth to know that the source of the pressure he felt on his chest would have been nice to explore more fully. He had completely forgotten what it felt like to have a tight throat when he looked into someone else's eyes. He could never tell Cherise, but the evening had been just a little more than Wally could handle.

The Writer

Once again, he was glad that Kelly had been there to take care of things.

CHAPTER EIGHT

BANG BANG – ZOOM ZOOM: SOMETHING ELSE TO WRITE ABOUT

It had been a long week. Wally had filled his tablet with observations about people and fantasies about what they were doing. The exercise had actually started to have an effect. Wally felt that he was more creative. He was letting his mind explore areas that he had previously put down as being off limits. Cargo vans that came past his toll booth were no longer carrying two plumbers going to a job on the other side of the bay. They were drug smugglers. The man in the business suit was a con artist. The woman with two kids in the back seat was a single mom on her way to drop the kids at grandma's house before she went out to commit suicide. The happy couple in the brand new sports car had just won the lottery. They were driving to the port where they would catch a cruise ship to the Caribbean. Another mom was dropping off her three children at summer camp so that she and her husband could have a romantic week alone.

The problem of how to create fantasies was being solved. But the problem of writing about them remained. Wally had never done any plumbing or driven a van. He'd certainly never smuggled anything. He'd never used drugs, conned any one, considered

The Writer

suicide, been to summer camp, or spent a romantic week with a woman.

Slowly, these thoughts of *never did that* gave way to thoughts of his recent experiences. He had gone on a cruise. It was only a dinner cruise, but it was a cruise. He had driven a brand new sports car, even if he hadn't bought it. The happiest thought was that he had never entertained thoughts of suicide even though his life had not been the best. Wally knew that there must be something more to him and he was going to find it and drag it to the surface. He would start this weekend. He would start today. Wally was taking Kelly to the gun shop. He was going to buy Kelly a gun and get shooting lessons.

Walter dutifully recorded these thoughts in his tablet while having his morning coffee. He might need them later when it was time to write something into a novel. When he finished, he cleaned up, got on his scooter, and headed out into the world. He was going to give Kelly something to write about.

The man in the gun shop welcomed Walter with a big smile. Shop owners could tell in an instant who had walked into their store. There were people with an air of confidence, people with almost no air at all, and a whole list of categories in between. The confident ones were usually ex-military, police, or rural Americans who were already experienced. They didn't usually need a salesman as much as they needed someone to reach what they needed, ring it up, and bag it. The people at the other end of the spectrum were wide-eyed, uncertain, and often appeared timid. They had come into the shop as a result of some incident that had finally convinced them that maybe owning a firearm wasn't really a bad idea. These were the people that needed help. Some shop owners saw them as an easy sale, but most saw them as someone

The Writer

who really shouldn't own a gun until they got the proper training and started moving down the scale towards the first group.

Wally was in this group.

"Hello!" Mark said. "Can I help you?"

Wally didn't say anything for a few seconds. He wasn't sure what to say. Mark knew this. He'd seen it a hundred times before and he waited patiently for his new customer to find his tongue.

"I've never been in a gun shop before," Wally finally said in a somewhat subdued manner.

"Why are you here now?" Mark asked, countering Wally's timid tone with an upbeat one and a smile.

"I want to get some experience. I've never shot a gun and I just want to know what it feels like."

"Okay," Mark said, coming around from behind the counter. "What you might consider is taking a class. We have an introductory class starting in about ten minutes, so your timing is good."

"A class?" Wally asked.

"Yes, sir," Mark replied. "What we do is go through how a gun works and gun safety in a classroom. At the end of the two hour course, we take you into our indoor range and let you fire three different handguns. We start with a small caliber one so that you get the feel of it. Then, after you're comfortable, we give you a medium caliber gun, and then a heavier one. It's all very safe and at the end of it, you'll have a bit of an education and a bit of shooting experience."

"What's it cost?" Wally asked.

The Writer

"It's fifty dollars but if you buy a gun, today or any time in the next three months, we apply it to the purchase price." Mark smiled.

Wally agreed and Kelly took a seat at a table in the classroom. There were four other students. There was a married couple in their early sixties who had decided to take home-protection both more seriously and more personally. The other two were college students. Two young girls, away from home for the first time and more than a little concerned about their personal safety, had decided to take the course to find their limits.

Mark taught the course himself. He was very thorough. He began by explaining how a cartridge worked. It wasn't a bullet. The bullet was the part that flew out of the end of the gun. The cartridge was the combination of the brass case, the bullet, the powder, and that little round dimple that the firing pin struck to make it go off. That was the primer. When the primer was hit by the firing pin, the unstable chemical inside it exploded. There wasn't much in there. But it was just enough to light off the gunpowder. When the solid gunpowder turned to gas as it burned, the pressure inside the cartridge built up until it was enough to break the bullet free of where it was seated at the open end of the shell casing. That was the brass part. The whole thing wouldn't be much more than a big firecracker if the cartridge wasn't in the steel chamber of the firearm. The only way out – for the gas – was down the barrel. To get out, the gas had to push the bullet out. By the time the bullet had gone the five inches to the end of the barrel, it was traveling at anywhere from 900 to 1,500 feet per second. Different handguns were manufactured for different velocities.

The next topic in the class was gun safety. Most things were pretty obvious. Never point the gun at anything you don't intend to shoot. Always assume that a gun is loaded. Never put your finger

The Writer

on the trigger until you're ready to shoot. Never leave a weapon where an untrained person can get it.

Mark encapsulated it well, "In spite of the inherently obvious nature of these rules, breaking them is the one and only cause of accidental death by firearms."

That part stunned both Walter and Kelly. Walter determined to search the internet to find out if it was true. Kelly accepted it and eagerly awaited Mark's next topic.

Pulling several blue plastic fake guns out of a bin, Mark handed one to each person at the table. For the next five minutes, they would handle the fake guns and Mark would observe their behavior, correcting things that he saw them doing wrong. He had them pass the guns to each other and watched as they transferred the fake firearms to see that they did so in a safe manner.

When he was satisfied, he said, "Okay. Everyone please stand up and come to this side of the table." With the five students lined up on one side of the cafeteria style table, he continued the lesson in safety. "Let's say that this table is the firing line. Over there are your targets." Mark pointed to the wall opposite the table. "What we'll do now is to go through range safety. Put your weapon on the table and take a step back. When I say so, I want you to take a step up, pick up your weapon, and take aim at the target."

Everyone nodded, indicating that they understood. "Okay. Go," Mark said.

The five students took a step forward and picked up their blue hard plastic guns. The elderly man took a shooting stance as if he had done this at least once before. His wife picked up the gun and pointed it at the wall. One of the college girls dropped hers and the other one turned to look at her and laugh.

The Writer

"Freeze," Mark commanded. Starting with the laughing college girl, he pointed out that when she turned to laugh, she ended up pointing the plastic gun at her friend's stomach. Her finger was on the trigger. The girl who had dropped her gun had picked it up wrapping all her fingers around the butt. Then when she tried to adjust her grip to free one finger to use on the trigger, she lost control. The elderly woman had picked up the weapon and was pointing it at the target, but she too had her finger already on the trigger. She was holding it in a way that would end up getting her finger cut when the slide came back to eject the shell. Kelly had put his finger on the trigger, but had remembered at the last second and removed it.

Mark patiently corrected each person and the exercise was repeated until he was satisfied that each one had learned the lesson. He then collected the plastic guns and set out real handguns on the table in front of the shooters. Each person received two weapons. Each had a revolver and a semi-automatic.

"Are these guns loaded?" Mark asked. Everyone nodded except the elderly woman.

"You wouldn't give us loaded guns," she said.

"I can make a mistake," Mark countered.

Mark walked each of the students through the process of loading and unloading each type of firearm using blanks. He explained how each one worked and what the benefits of each style were. Then there was a repeat of the range safety exercise, picking up and pointing the weapon at the target.

When he had explained the difference between pointing and aiming a firearm and was satisfied with the other lessons, he said, "Okay. Let's go to the range and shoot!"

57

The Writer

Kelly enjoyed the experience at the range. Each shooter had their own spot on the firing line. Between each shooting station was a vertical wall. Shells that were ejected from one pistol bounced off the wall instead of hitting the adjacent shooter in the head. Mark was very patient. At first each shooter was allowed to load only one round into the firearm at a time. When the shooter had become comfortable, Mark allowed two rounds. After 30 minutes, all the shooters were loading full magazines of between 8 and 15 rounds and firing at will. One of the girls had a hard time at first, but she got used to it thanks to Mark's watchful eye and careful corrections.

Kelly found the smell to be especially pleasant. He'd never smelled gunpowder before and he found that he liked it. He also liked the fact that he could choose a weapon that suited him. He was small and had weak arms. Kelly cursed Wally for not at least trying to work out a little. The .22 caliber revolver felt good to him. But he knew it was too small to give him the experience that he wanted. The .38 was bigger and heavier. Kelly could hold it and aim it, but if he didn't fire it within two or three seconds, he had to put it down and start over. The barrel would just start wobbling all over the place as his arm tired. The .45 was actually a little easier. It weighed about the same as the .38, but the barrel was shorter and that made it a little easier to keep it aimed. The kick, however, was too much. Kelly finally settled on a Walther .380 as the right gun for him. The .380 fired a bullet that was the same diameter as the .38, but it was much less powerful. The weapon itself was smaller and weighed about half of what the .38 did. It was perfect.

After filling out the forms to complete the purchase, Kelly learned that he would need to wait 3 days before he took it home. Mark assured him, however, that if he wanted to come in and practice, the weapon would be at the store and he could use it at the range. The surprise came when Mark offered to sign him up for a concealed weapon license.

"Can I do that?" Kelly asked. "I just learned to shoot the thing today. I think I missed the target about half the time."

"The law says that I have to certify that you know how to use the firearm properly." Mark smiled. "It doesn't say anything about being able to use it well. Of course, I do recommend lots and lots of practice. That's why you get five free range days with the purchase."

"Okay," Kelly agreed. "Let's do that."

Wally paid the annual membership fee to the range and also looked into the more advanced and specialized classes. They were patterned after the training that police took, but Wally guessed that they were really supposed to be for fun.

"Not always." Kelly corrected Wally. "That action shooting course is for fun but it also feeds the egos of cop wannabes." Walter accepted the correction. Under normal circumstances, there would be no reason for a private citizen to want to run down a plywood alley shooting bad guys and holding their fire when faced with a little girl. It was like a live-fire video game.

After Kelly left, Walter stayed at the shop and got extra training in how to clean and care for the weapon that he had selected. He purchased a couple of boxes of ammunition, a cleaning kit, and a guide to shooting safety before he returned to his apartment.

After lunch Walter and Kelly scoured the internet for more experiences to add to the things that Kelly could write about. Referring back to the list that Wally had made earlier, they finally

The Writer

settled on an excursion that had something to do with driving fast cars. The experience at the dealership was nice, but it was too controlled. Walter thought that Kelly needed something more exhilarating and less dangerous to the general public. A while ago, Wally had learned that some race tracks offer a theme-park style experience for people. Paying customers were allowed to drive real race cars on the actual tracks used in competition. It was an immensely popular, if somewhat expensive, way to spend a Sunday afternoon. A few clicks and an online payment later, Walter had made reservations at the local race track. The most difficult part of the process was learning how to buy something online.

When Walter arrived at the track and checked in, he was almost overwhelmed by the raw power that seemed to permeate the area. The track was closed. There were no races scheduled. Only a few race cars were visible on trailers in the parking lot and a few more were being worked on in the garage but the place was still almost oppressive. The track shop was small and unassuming, but the garage was huge. It smelled of grease, gasoline, and specialty cleaning fluids. The echoes in the garage lent a surrealistic air to the experience. It was too much. Wally was not going to be able to handle it.

"That's okay," Kelly said. "I got this. I was going to drive anyway, so I'll go ahead and take over now."

Wally faded into oblivion and Kelly listened intently as the instructor showed him the inside of the stock car that he would be driving. It was supposed to be a Ford Mustang, but the only stock item left was the frame and the shell of the body. The interior had been fitted with a roll cage and bucket seats. Almost everything else had been removed. The engine was stock, but had been tweaked in accordance with NASCAR guidelines. The instructor

The Writer

found a helmet that fit Kelly and then gave him a jump suit and told him to go change.

Once they got to the car that Kelly would actually drive, the instructor showed Kelly to the passenger seat. Before customers were allowed to drive, they needed to know what it felt like to go fast. Kelly thought it odd that it was the same step-by-step approach that the gun dealer used. Then he realized that neither the firearm instructor nor the driving instructor was interested in dying. The slow introduction to a dangerous sport was essential in overcoming fear but it was also essential in creating a familiarity that would allow the shooter or the driver to react well in previously unfamiliar situations.

The instructor strapped Kelly in, took his place behind the wheel, and started out on the track. With each circuit he increased the speed of the car. Starting at 100 mph he made 8 circuits. During the final straightaway, traveling at 180 mph, the instructor shoved the gas pedal to the floor. The car jumped ahead enough to push Kelly back into the seat. He was amazed that there was so much power left at that speed. At the finish line, they were travelling just under 200 mph.

The instructor took one more lap just to slow down and let Kelly's heart rate return to something near normal. "Your turn," he announced when they pulled into the pit.

Kelly hesitated, but only for a moment. The two men traded places and Kelly eased the car out onto the track. His first lap would not be at 100 mph. On the straightaway, Kelly pushed the speed up to about 80, but in the curves, he slowed to almost 50. On the second lap, he managed to push his top speed up, but still slowed dramatically for the curves.

The Writer

"If you slow too fast as you enter the curve, you can lose traction and slide," the instructor warned Kelly. "It's really better to slow just before the curve and maintain or increase your speed once you're in the curve."

Kelly pushed the car to 110, slowed to 65 for the upcoming curve, and pressed lightly on the gas when he entered it. Exiting the curve at 75 mph, he then increased speed on the next straightaway. After ten laps, he was hitting 150 mph and slowing to 95 in the curve. What struck Kelly most about this experience was the steering. It was tight. The Alpha Romeo handled easily. The race car wore him out. He realized that driving a race car took a lot more arm strength and muscular endurance than he'd ever imagined. The totality of the concentration surprised him too. It wasn't oppressive or scary. In fact, Kelly found it liberating. He didn't think about what he would have for dinner or what new experience Wally would send him on next weekend. Girls paying tolls and Lisa the saleslady were no longer strutting around in the back of his mind. He no longer had a back to his mind at all. There was nothing but the upcoming curve and the need to control the car.

The Writer

CHAPTER NINE

UP, UP AND AWAY!

Throughout the entire week, Walter had dutifully recorded mini-stories about the people who passed through the lane at his toll booth. On Friday night, situated in his understuffed chair with his beer and microwave dinner, he reviewed his work. It didn't take him long to reassure himself that his plan was working.

A few weeks ago, Wally had tried to write nothing more elaborate than plot summaries. He hadn't even gotten to the point of attempting an actual outline. A dinner cruise, a dance, a fast car, a day at the range, and a day at the track later, the fantasies he recorded on his tablet had changed dramatically.

The truck driver that had gone through on Tuesday had been hauling brand new Porsches. Instead of being delivered to the dealership on the other side of the bay, Wally imagined that they were being delivered to the race track for modification. The guy in the next car was no longer a realtor on his way to show a house like the sign on his car indicated. He was the test driver for one of the cars on the truck ahead. He wanted to be a race car driver, but had to pay his dues. His job was to work with the mechanics as they altered this and modified that to convert the stock model into a NASCAR model.

The Writer

The sexy brunette in the next car was no longer on vacation from Utah. She was the girl that the test driver saw every night to release the tension of driving race cars all day. The middle aged woman in the next car was not on her way to buy her husband a birthday present at the mall. She was the wife of the race car driver who would eventually drive the Porsche that was on the first truck. She had learned that the younger girl was not only sleeping with the test driver, but she was also sleeping with her husband. Later that night, she was going to kill the little slut. In her head, she knew that ten years ago she had been the young slut working her way up in the driver's circuit but she tried to deny it. Her plan was to somehow get the little bitch alone when they were on the dinner cruise later that night. She would shoot her with her brand new revolver and toss her body overboard. As an afterthought, she added that if her husband got in the way, she'd shoot him too.

What made Wally feel so good about his new scenario was not that he was able to put little vignettes together. He had done that when Brandon shot the cowboy and dragged Gail away to rape her. What made Wally feel good was that Kelly now knew exactly what it felt like to try and dance on a wooden dance floor that rolled slightly with the motion of the ship. Kelly knew the smell of gunpowder and would be able to describe in great detail what it felt like to point a gun at something and pull the trigger. He could write about the weight of the weapon and how it moved in his hand. He would find the right words to make the reader hear the crack of the shot and see the fire emerge from the end of the barrel and disappear in a microsecond. Kelly could describe the test drive, the acceleration, the caution and skill needed to enter a curve at high speed, the constant arm-numbing fight with the steering wheel combined with the light, almost artistic, touch of feet on the gas

The Writer

and brake pedals. Wally recalled his night with Tiffany in college and realized that he himself could supply the detail about what it meant to have meaningless sex.

Walter knew that these experiences were still not enough for Kelly to be able to write a novel, but they were a start. Tomorrow, Walter would take Kelly to the airport.

Skydiving, Walter said to himself.

Maneuvering his scooter into a spot that said *motorcycles only* outside the private section of the small regional airport, Wally wondered what the hell he was doing.

"You're giving me stuff to write about." Kelly admonished him to stay focused on why there were there. "Remember? I can't write about something I don't know about." With a streak of meanness, unanticipated on Wally's part, Kelly added, "And you're too chicken to do it yourself."

Walter had to think about that. Was he really too scared for this stuff? Why had he started this project in the first place? He put it aside. He would need to think about that later. There was work to do.

Inside the small building, Wally found himself in the company of five other would-be sky divers. He wanted to take notes on them just like he did in his toll booth, but he couldn't. He didn't have his tablet and he couldn't focus. Maybe Kelly was right. Maybe he was scared.

The instructor went through an orientation, telling the six students (seven if you count Kelly) exactly what would happen. They would take off, climb to 12,000 feet, circle a big field that

The Writer

wasn't far away, and jump. Each of them would be firmly secured to an instructor. All the student had to do was jump.

"If you have to close your eyes, go ahead," the man said. "If you need to hold something, hold your own hands in front of your chest. Do not try and turn around and hang onto the instructor. He is attached to you by straps and clps and all you'll do is twist yourselves around. If you are good to go, signal with a thumbs-up when you are in the door. If you cecide not to jump, hold up a fist. Your instructor will ease you back away from the door. There's only one thing we don't want you to do." He paused. "Please don't puke."

The students laughed. The instructors laughed. Assistants appeared from nowhere and began fitting each of them with jump suits, helmets, goggles, and ear plugs to dampen the noise. Off to the side of the room was a mock-up of the interior of an airplane. It was equipped with seats and a door so that students could walk through the steps of standing up, getting hooked up, and standing in the door in preparation for their jump.

Wally realized that this was just like the track and the range. Even a little familiarity could go a long way in improving safety. Somewhere in the back of his mird something clicked. All the times that he had been told as a kid that he shouldn't touch this or couldn't use that, whether it was a bicycle, the stove, or a power drill, he had been denied that familiarity. Later on, these same things would bring trepidation, if not fear, when he was forced to use them. Maybe these early experiences had been the first building blocks of his fortress of low self-esteem. Maybe he would tell Kelly about it later. Maybe Kelly would work that into a story.

The Writer

It was time to go. The seven students and seven instructors walked across the hot tarmac towards the jump plane. The twin-engine aircraft had already been warmed up by the pilot. The engine away from the door was turning slowly while the propeller on the side that they approached from had been feathered. The engine was turning, but it had been disengaged from the propeller to reduce any possibility that a student might get hurt.

The group climbed on board, each student sitting next to their designated instructor. Kelly, for all his personality traits that were the opposite of Walter's, was still a small man and he had been paired with a young woman. The instructor had said that it had something to do with aerodynamics and safety and that Kelly shouldn't be insulted. Oddly, it had not occurred to either Kelly or Wally to be insulted until the instructor mentioned it.

The take-off was smooth. The air was smooth. The flight was smooth.

The instructor had told them that the day was perfect for a first jump. The winds were calm at the surface and aloft. The sun was shining and all was right with the world. He was apparently right in his assessment. Up until the moment that he signaled that it was time for the first student to stand and hook into his instructor, everything went perfectly. The first student-instructor pair hobbled to the door. The instructor's arms, extended to the side, held the frame firmly as he waited for his student to give him the thumbs-up signal.

When he did, the student and the instructor calmly leaned forward and half stepped and half fell out of the door. Two students later, it was Kelly's turn. He stood up, hooked up, and moved to the door. Crossing his arms in front of himself, he stared

The Writer

out into the nothingness. He was going to puke. He wasn't going to puke. He was going to pee. He controlled that too. He was going to puke again. No. He forced himself not to puke. Everything below was so small. He was so high. The wind was smacking him around. The wind buffeted the cloth from the jump suit and buffeted what little courage he had mustered in his soul. After standing in the door for at least two full minutes, he held up a fist. The instructor eased him back inside, unhooked him, and guided him back to a seat.

While the other students dutifully took their turns standing, hooking up, and jumping, Kelly's instructor did everything she could to calm him down. She made solid eye contact, smiled, stroked his arm in a comforting but not condescending way and assured him that no one was going to toss him out of the plane. It was her joke that finally broke Kelly's fear and gave him the strength to try again. A little more slowly this time, he stood up. She clipped them together and they walked to the door. This time, although he wanted to hold up a fist again, he found his thumb extended upwards. He could feel his instructor lean against his back. He could feel her use her knee at the back of his leg to encourage him to lift his foot. Out of the corner of his eye, he saw her release the side of the door. Kelly fell out of the aircraft and plummeted to earth.

Suddenly, he was no longer afraid. He no longer felt the urge to puke. Free fall involved a lot of wind and his jump suit flapped furiously, but the noise of the airplane was gone. Once his stomach had caught up with the rest of his body, he no longer had the feeling that he was falling. He was floating. The flapping of his jump suit reminded him that he was floating rapidly, but it was no longer frightening. This wonderful experience lasted for a little over forty-

The Writer

five seconds and then his instructor deployed the parachute. Kelly had expected a sharp snap as the cloth captured the wind and pulled the pair almost to a halt. Instead of a jerk, he felt a smooth increase in upward pressure on his harness. He had been told that the new rig contained a shock absorber – now he knew what that meant. Hanging there in front of his instructor, even the buffeting of his jump suit had quieted. It was quiet. It was really, really quiet.

Kelly looked out over the landscape in awe. With the fear completely gone, he was able to experience the beauty and solitude of the experience. He knew that he wasn't completely alone, but there was still a solitude that was nothing short of inspiring.

The feeling lasted until he got close enough to the pasture below that he could once again detect the motion associated with the jump. The ground was coming up. He was falling down. Relativity didn't matter. There was going to be a bump. He remembered the instruction. He remembered the practice landings that he had done in the mockup. Knees bent slightly. Feet together. His only job was to avoid hurting himself. The instructor would take most of the impact of landing.

The wind in Wally's face as he rode his scooter back to his apartment was no longer bothersome. For a long time, the wind had been the only thing about his scooter that he didn't really like. After his experience in free fall, the 50 mph wind that resulted from his ride was a gentle breeze. It was the relativity of the experiences that stuck in Wally's mind. He had never fired a gun until one day he fired a small, medium, and large caliber gun in one day. Now that he had his .380 and was used to it, the smaller .22 seemed insignificant. He'd never driven faster than 55 mph until his test ride with Lisa. He'd never driven faster than 95 mph. Last week he had guided a high-powered vehicle at 190 mph. Today, 55 seemed painfully slow.

Wally unlocked the door to the apartment, went in, and stared out the window overlooking the quadrangle below. Only this morning, the view from his third floor window seemed like it was from on high. After falling 5,000 feet, it seemed unimpressive.

Sifting through the course of the events of the day, there was only one thing that Wally found unexplainable. For some reason skydiving had made him horny. Wally wanted to get laid.

"Well," Kelly argued. "Getting laid is on your list of things that exciting people do."

Wally nodded in assent.

"So? Are we doing that or not?" Kelly pressed the point, angering Walter.

"What do you want me to do?" Wally was at a loss for ideas. "Hire a hooker?"

"Why not?" Kelly countered.

"Dumbass," Wally replied. "Truly exciting people don't pay for it. If you want to get laid, you're going to have to convince someone."

"You could call Cherise." Kelly grinned smugly.

Walter was exasperated. "Just leave it alone! Please?"

With that, Kelly went away and Wally went to the tablet to record the experiences of the day. He wanted to get it all down before he went to bed so that the memories and emotions would be fresh. Tomorrow, Sunday, he had something else planned and he didn't want his reactions to get mixed up with each other.

The Writer

He did take the time, however, when he finished his notes to do a brief internet search on the relationship between doing exciting things, like skydiving, and sexual arousal. It didn't take long before he learned that the increased respiration rate, pulse rate, and blood pressure released some of the same hormones and set off some of the same reactions that were involved in sexual intercourse. He took a few notes and set the research aside. Maybe Kelly could use it in a story someday.

Walter and Kelly were back at the same airport at 9:00 AM the next day. This time it was for an introductory lesson in flying. The instructor was not much more than a kid. Or so it seemed to Walter. Barely 30 years old, their instructor had learned to fly and had served well during his ten years in the Air Force. He had wanted to make a career out of it, but a freak accident had cost him his big toe. Unable to fly fighter jets, he had decided to resign his commission and go into private practice.

"Good morning!" the man said cheerily as Walter entered the flight school office. "I'm Tink Miller, and we're ready to go if you are!" Kelly agreed and after Wally had signed a few waivers, Tink led the way to the aircraft. It was a single engine airplane in a configuration that Tink called *high wing*. What that meant was that the wing was attached to the fuselage at the top of the cabin, not at the bottom. Tink showed Kelly around the plane, describing the parts and explaining what they did. He painstakingly went over every flight surface, wiggling the flaps, ailerons, and rudder to make sure that they were in working order. Tink explained that what he was doing was called a pre-flight check and that it was incredibly important to assure the safety of the upcoming flight. Wally made a mental note about instructors using familiarity to reduce stress.

The Writer

Once inside and buckled in, Tink continued his orientation. He pointed out the gauges and dials explaining what each one did and showed Kelly how to adjust his headset. The only thing that really seemed important was that Kelly not grab the yoke and that he not put his feet on the rudder pedals. Tink assured him that when the time came, if he continued with the lessons, he would get ample opportunity to work the controls.

Tink asked if Kelly was ready and when he nodded, Tink moved the throttle forward and pressed a red button on the left side of the console. The propeller turned slowly, the groan of an electric motor accentuating the strain. Then there was a bang, a pause, another bang, another pause, and then a sudden sequence of bangs which eventually merged into the sound of a propeller driven aircraft engine.

Tink adjusted a few knobs and contacted the control tower. Kelly could hear the transmission in his headset. *This is cool*, he thought to himself.

A mechanic from the flight school came out of the hanger and, using hand signals, Tink asked him to remove the wheel chocks. Ten seconds later, the mechanic held the wooden blocks up for Tink to see and waved. Tink waited until the man was a safe distance away before easing the throttle forward and releasing the brakes. Slowly, the aircraft began to roll. Suddenly there were two short jerks. Kelly was startled. Walter was afraid.

Tink's voice came through the headset. "Just testing the brakes. It's better to know that they work now than to find out they don't work sometime later when you really need them."

Kelly smiled and nodded.

The Writer

Tink eased the airplane to the end of the runway and pushed the throttle all the way to the stop. As the plane gained speed, Tink pointed to the gauge that showed RPMs and said, "When we get to this point, I'll pull the throttle back again. We don't want to overspeed the engine." Neither Wally nor Kelly had any idea what overspeeding the engine meant, but it didn't sound good. Kelly would ask about it later. At the moment, he didn't want to distract Tink from his take-off.

The weather was just like it had been yesterday. Clear and calm, there was no sign of any storms and the tops of the palm trees didn't show any sign of a breeze.

Tink pointed to the control panel again. "When we get to 90 knots, I'm going to lift the nose just a tiny bit and we'll come up off the ground."

Kelly watched the needle creep up to 90. Tink moved the yoke back only about an inch and the nose of the airplane angled up slightly, after which Tink moved the yoke back to where it had been before. Almost at exactly the same time, Kelly felt the wheels lose contact with the runway. Tink pulled a green handled lever located between the seats and the sound of a motor grinding somewhere beneath his feet told Kelly that the landing gear was coming up. When the sound of the motor stopped, Kelly could feel that the air flowed more smoothly over the skin of the plane. There was not as much vibration and buffeting as there had been only seconds earlier.

"How come you pulled the yoke back and then pushed it forward again?" Kelly asked.

The Writer

"Very observant!" Tink said. "You see, when I pull it back, the elevators[1] on the tail bend up. That makes the plane want to pitch nose-up. Once I was pointed in the right direction, I had to put the yoke back to the center, or we would have continued to turn up instead of flying up in a straight line; we'd do a loop."

Tink held that position for a minute or two and then pushed the yoke forward until the plane leveled off.

Pulling the yoke back again to the starting point he said, "See there? I had to push over to get level, but once level, I had to center the elevator again. Watch the tip of the wing." Kelly looked out the window and up at the tip of the wing. Tink twisted the yoke slightly to the right and Kelly saw the aileron move up. "With that little guy canted up like that the wing is forced down." Tink centered the yoke again and the aileron lined up again with the wing. "If I put her in a bank or a turn and leave her there, we just continue to turn. If I kept that thing bent up, we'd end up doing a roll."

The lesson went on in much the same manner for about thirty minutes. Tink would do something and let Kelly see the effect. He pulled the throttle back and shoved it forward. Kelly could feel the shift in his weight as he slowed or accelerated. Climbing and diving could be felt as a little more or a little less weight in Kelly's stomach.

"That feeling is because your guts actually kind of float inside you. They aren't firmly attached like an arm or a leg," Tink explained.

Kelly was enjoying the ride but it seemed sort of boring. "How fast are we going?" he asked.

---

[1] The elevator is the bendable part of the horizontal tail stabilizer that goes up or down when the stick is pulled back or pushed forward.

The Writer

"Three hundred knots," Tink answered.

"How fast is that really?" Kelly had no idea what a knot was if it wasn't in his shoestring.

"About three forty-five, I guess," Tink answered. "In miles per hour."

"It doesn't seem that fast," Kelly said.

"You've got no frame of reference," Tink explained. "If we were ten feet off the ground, then you could tell very easily. If we had a cloud to fly through, I could show you."

"That's okay," Kelly said. "I believe you. It's still kind of boring."

"There's an old saying." Tink laughed. "Flying is hours and hours of total boredom occasionally interrupted by a few seconds of stark terror."

Unexplainably, Tink laughed again. "Why don't you try it? I need some terror today!"

"Seriously?" Kelly asked.

"Yeah." Tink grinned at Kelly. "You take the yoke but just hold it. Don't do anything unless I ask you to."

"Okay." Kelly put his hands on the yoke.

Tink took his hands away from the controls and placed them on his knees.

"I'll still work the rudder, so keep your feet pulled back," he said. "Now wait till I say so, then just tilt the yoke ever so slightly to the left, count to three, and then put it back in the middle."

Kelly nodded.

The Writer

"Ready?" Tink asked.

Kelly nodded again.

"Okay. Go," Tink instructed.

Kelly rocked the yoke slowly until he felt something move, counted to three, and put it back in the middle. The airplane had slowly banked left and then stayed there when Kelly re-centered the yoke.

"Okay! Good job!" Tink said. "Now make her level again."

Kelly moved the yoke slowly to the right and held it as the plane leveled off, then moved the yoke back to where it belonged.

"You're a natural!" Tink exclaimed.

It had been a while since Wally had made his presence known, but now he said to Kelly, "He's just trying to sell you $6,000 worth of flying lessons."

Several hours later in his understuffed chair, Wally completed his notes on the day: *Kelly said that the only thing that really looked hard was the landing.*

Walter looked at what he wrote. He thought it was odd that he had referred to Kelly in the third person. Kelly was serving a purpose; there was no doubt about that. But Walter needed to keep things in perspective. He deleted it and wrote it over: *The only thing that was really hard about flying was the landing. Landing itself wasn't hard. Looking at an airfield from 3,000 feet and trying to figure out how to aim the plane and descend at the right rate so that you ended up positioned a hundred feet above the end of the runway when you passed over it was the hard part.*

The Writer

Wally nodded to himself. The rest was easy. Flaps down, gear down, set up a slow descent rate, pull off some of the power at five to ten feet, settle into the runway, pull the rest of the power off, lightly apply the brakes, and steer to the parking spot.

Walter looked through the status board he had created for Kelly's development. He was going to have to ask Jack for some vacation time.

CHAPTER TEN

SAINT THOMAS

"Good morning, Jack," Walter said as he came into the office on Monday morning. "I think I'll need some time off."

Jack was surprised, but happy. "Wally!" he exclaimed from behind his desk. "You've taken a total of four sick days and three vacation days in 18 years. Are you sure?"

Wally nodded, "Yeah. I'm sure. How much time do I have?"

Jack called up the computer file where he kept PTO records. "Well, we cashed in last year like we usually do, so you have about three weeks available right now."

"Oh," Wally said. "I forgot about that. What was the exchange on the cash in?"

"It's one day's pay for two days of sick time and two days' pay for three days of straight vacation time." Jack examined Wally's file. "Last year we converted the maximum balance and deposited about $1,800 into your account. The year before you had hit the limit and we had to convert a lot more. That year we deposited … mmm … let's see … here it is. $3,800." Jack looked up at Wally. "You goin' somewhere?"

The Writer

Wally blinked, not wanting to reveal his plans. "I think I'd like two weeks off. It doesn't matter when. You can make it fit into the schedule whenever it's convenient for you."

Jack loved that about Wally and he hated it at the same time. He really liked that Wally wasn't a pushy employee and understood the upheaval that two weeks of vacation could cause. He really hated the fact that Wally didn't have much need for vacation in the first place.

"I'll make it work," he said. "Everything's okay, isn't it?" Jack was genuinely concerned. "I mean no one's sick or something, are they?" As he asked, Jack realized that he didn't even know if Wally had family or not.

"It's okay," Wally said softly. "I just decided to take a trip."

"Where're you off to?" Jack asked.

"I thought I'd go to St. Thomas," Wally replied. "You know, down in the Caribbean?"

Jack grinned and said, "All-righty then! We're gonna make this happen! Tell you what. I'll sandwich it between weekends so you can get a total of 18 days in a row!"

"That'd be great," Wally replied with almost no enthusiasm at all.

Walter Fleegle spent the next week putting together the itinerary for his trip. Jack had pulled a few strings and made the time off appear almost as if by magic. In truth, he had offered some of the other attendants overtime so that Wally could go right away. It seemed that everyone liked Wally, but he was so quiet that no one had ever become friends with him.

The Writer

The week after that, Wally said goodbye to Jack at 4:30 Friday afternoon promising that he would be back in time for work and well rested in 19 days. Jack wished him the best of luck and said that if he needed anything that he should call.

Wally nodded. It was nice to know that there was someone willing to even promise such a thing. Wally knew Jack would live up to the promise and that was even nicer.

At home, Wally collected his bags and waited for the taxi. He could have asked Jack for a ride. He knew that now. But making his own way had become such a habit that it didn't really matter. Wally took the taxi to the airport and caught a late flight to San Juan. It was nearly midnight when he arrived. Consuela Mayaguez, the counter clerk at the Holiday Inn, was expecting him and he was promptly escorted to a very comfortable room. It was odd, he thought, that the room at the Holiday Inn was almost as big as his efficiency apartment.

In the morning, Wally was up at nine. He was just in time to take advantage of the free continental breakfast before finding the concierge.

"Good morning, sir." The man with the gold nametag greeted Walter cheerily. Apparently his name was Billy De Moines. Walter thought that it was a funny name until he realized that the moniker *Billy De Moines* had been constructed in the same way that *Consuela Mayaguez* had been. The name on the tag was a combination of the actual first name and the city where the person lived before being hired. Apparently hotels think that makes them more cosmopolitan. It didn't matter.

"Good morning," Walter said. "I need to make connections with Sun Charters."

The Writer

"Certainly, sir." Billy picked up the telephone. "I'll call them."

Half an hour later, Walter tipped Billy and climbed into the shuttle from the sailing charter service. He was going to be one of twelve passengers and two crewmen leaving that afternoon for the islands of St. Thomas and St. John in the US Virgin Islands.

Wally was the last one to arrive at the dock. The 70 foot McKinley ketch was a beautiful ship. As soon as he saw her, Walter decided that it would be disrespectful to call her a sailboat. She was a sailing ship. There were two masts, which is what made her a ketch. One was well forward while the other was located aft of the cockpit where the wheel and controls were located. Spike, the mate, collected Walter's bags and took them below while the Captain welcomed Walter along with the other guests.

"We'll be leaving shortly," Captain Jeffries announced. "All I ask at this time is that you stay in this area here ..." he gestured to the cockpit. "... or on the aft deck or below until we get out of the harbor. This is a very busy time on a sailing vessel. Once we clear the sea buoy, we'll go over a few do's and don'ts before we settle in for the voyage. The weather is good and we should be in Charlotte Amalie, St. Thomas, in about 14 hours."

Walter looked around at the other eleven people. He decided that maybe this wasn't such a good idea. He'd always had his space and his privacy. Twelve passengers on a 70 foot ship allowed for a little less than six feet per person, he told himself. As his anxiety rose in him like an unwanted guest, so did Kelly Blanton.

"Go hide somewhere, ya big pansy." Kelly mocked Wally. Standing on the aft deck, as far back as he could go without falling overboard, Kelly surveyed the ship. Behind him, hanging off the back of the ship on a couple of small davits, was a little skiff. Kelly

The Writer

was leaning against a stainless steel rail that had been put there to keep people from falling overboard. Looking forward, he could see the Captain in the cockpit preparing to get under way. The aft deck was fairly large and two other passengers had decided to lean against the aft mast that rose from the deck between the cockpit and where Kelly stood.

Spike was running around tending lines and preparing the sails. Several of the passengers had decided that the best way to be out of the way was to go below. Other than Kelly and the couple just ahead of him, there were three others on deck. They had moved well forward and were sitting on the roof of the deck house that was located just forward of the cockpit. Kelly's attention turned back to the couple nearest to him. The man was easily in his late fifties. He had the kind of look that television shows liked to use as a stereotype for very wealthy, very healthy, older men. He was tallish, with close cropped gray hair. He was tanned, toned, and dressed in classic *rich old guy* style: white shorts, brown deck shoes, and a white polo shirt with red and blue stripes on the sleeve. Of course, he also wore one of those belts that had nautical flags emblazoned into a white background.

"Don't believe what you see." Wally warned Kelly. "If he was really that rich he wouldn't be on this charter. He'd own his own yacht."

Kelly conceded the point and turned his attention to the young lady with him. She also fulfilled a certain stereotype. She too was tanned and toned, sporting white shorts and a wispy cover-up that served to highlight rather than conceal her bikini clad chest. At first Kelly thought that she might be the old man's daughter. That was until he reached over and gave her ass a rub and a squeeze. The young woman didn't seem to mind at all.

The Writer

The three people up on the foredeck seemed to be a family. Mom, dad, and a teenage boy were enjoying the trip already. They joked with each other, although Kelly couldn't hear what was being said. It was clear that they were comfortable with each other. Kelly was happy for them.

Captain Jeffries completed his preparations and pushed a button on the console. Twin diesel engines located below deck sprang to life with a very subdued growl. Spike let go the mooring lines and the Captain put her into gear, pulling slowly away from the dock and into the harbor.

Slipping below, Kelly wanted to find his stateroom and let Wally make a few notes about the people on deck. On the way, he passed through the galley where the other six passengers were breaking out the booze. These happy six were the bridesmaids and groomsmen who had just sent their friends off on their honeymoon. There was money in the bride's family and the girl's father had decided to honor their participation with a voyage. His daughter had been aware of the pending gift, however, and, to avoid unintended consequences, the newlyweds had selected married couples for the wedding party.

In his cabin, Wally powered up the tablet and started to write.

"The Cruise." By Kelly Blanton.

Summary: Blake Billings turned fifty and he wasn't happy about it. Recently divorced as a result of his wife Shannon's dalliance with the tennis pro, he had lost almost everything. The fates smiled on him, though, and it wasn't a month after the divorce was

The Writer

final that he picked out a winning lottery ticket. It wasn't for big money, but it was enough that he wouldn't need to worry ever again – as long as he didn't blow it all. Blake always wanted to sail. He had worked hard for 25 years as a stock trader and had put away enough money to put his dream yacht within reach. That was the year his wife left. The winning lottery ticket wasn't enough to let him buy the $600,000 yacht that he wanted but it was enough to book a trip on one. It would have been a great trip in its own right, but Blake was still feeling vindictive. He decided to get even. Last year he had noticed a young girl at the gym who was really in good shape and very obviously a gold digger. She ignored all of the young men and came on to all of the middle-aged men – as long as they had driven to the gym in the right car, that is. Blake had seen through her game right away and had ignored her, but after the divorce, he let her play him like the big catch she was hoping to find. It wasn't long before he had purchased two berths on the charter sailing ship out of San Juan. For Blake, though, the best part – even better than the nightly romp – was posting pictures of him and her to his social media page. He was sure that his ex would see it all. Blake made sure of it by tagging her in the posts. All the photos of the gold digger were tagged as *not Shannon Billings*.

The Writer

Now what? Wally asked himself.

Walter considered tragedy. The young gold digger could have an accident and fall over the side. Blake could be charged with her murder? That might work, but a better story would be if the family man had been hired by the ex-wife to kill Blake. The wife and son could be a cover story. Maybe he would kill the gold digger too. Or maybe the Captain ... no ... Spike – the unlikely hero – could save the gold digger and reform her. She could see the error of her ways as a result of the brush with death and the two of them live happily ever after.

On the yacht? Wally reconsidered. Other ideas arose. Maybe the teenager's a drug user? Once in St. Thomas he gets caught up in the local underworld while trying to make a buy. Maybe he gets kidnapped. Then mom and dad could spend their vacation trying to find him and free him from bad guys. Of course the three couples from the wedding could end up in a drunken wife-swap party that leads to multiple deaths and problems.

Wally shook his head. More thoughts came to him. What if there was a shipwreck? Or a storm and some people were washed overboard? If the gold digger and the teenage boy ended up on an island together, it would make a good romance novel.

No, Wally told himself. He hated those things and wasn't going to let Kelly Blanton write one. They could all get shipwrecked. He dismissed the idea as being too reminiscent of Gilligan. It seemed like every plot he came up with had been done already by someone else. It stood to reason. With thousands of books being written every year, what made him think he could come up with something new?

The Writer

"What if Walter Fleegle commits suicide but he makes it look like a murder just so that his death would be more interesting than his life?" Kelly interrupted. "Then the story could be about how each of the passengers and crew becomes a suspect and is eventually cleared."

Wally turned off the power to the tablet and went to dinner with the rest of the passengers.

Everyone introduced themselves to each other as a prelude to dinner. Spike had served everyone a glass of wine and some cheese hors d'oeuvres to get things started. When it was Walter's turn, he gave them a short synopsis of life as a toll booth attendant, telling them that he was allowing himself a paid vacation before he retired. From then on, he was silent. He was collecting characters almost out of habit and found the need for the tablet to be less and less important. The wedding party babbled on about what a great time they had and how great it was for dad to give them this expensive trip. The little family turned out to be on a mission of rehabilitation, but it wasn't about drugs. A few months ago, the family had been a family of four, but the youngest a girl, had passed away of a sudden illness. Both mom and the teenage boy were having a hard time adjusting so the therapist advised them to create a memory that was just the three of them. They were working on it.

After dinner, Wally took his tablet topside and sat perched on the top of the main cabin, leaning against the mast. He could hear the wedding party in the galley drinking and talking happily. He couldn't fathom why they were inside instead of out here enjoying the night breeze, the moon, the stars, and the smell of the sea. On the bow, the family was doing exactly that. They had moved up into the bow pulpit and the teenage boy was doing his impression of

The Writer

that guy in the Titanic movie. He had both arms out to his side and was just enjoying the ride.

Walter Fleegle had decided that maybe Kelly Blanton had enough to start something serious. Wally started putting things together.

Twisted

Summary: [Note to author- Keep Brandon and Gail at the toll booth. They meet when the lady in the Cadillac gets the flat and drives off the side of the road. The cowboy helps, but he just changes the tire. Gail is still a nurse, but Brandon is now an off-duty paramedic. Brandon and Gail strike up a whirlwind romance that ends in marriage. Gail's dad sends the wedding party on a sailing excursion to St. Thomas in appreciation of the friendship and support that they had shown Gail over the years.]

The three couples from Gail and Brandon's wedding are joined on the cruise by a man suffering from a mid-life crisis, his sexy young companion, and a family of three. They head out of San Juan and make for Charlotte Amalie in St. Thomas. They are supposed to arrive in the early dawn hours but the Captain has a few too many glasses of rum and makes a mistake. He misses the course change that would take him south between Culebra and St. Thomas and ends up on the north side of St. Thomas instead of on

The Writer

the south side where the port of Charlotte Amalie is located.

Heaving to and tacking back into the wind, he fails to see the small uninhabited island that lies 4 miles north of West End. The sailing ship runs aground and breaks up on the rocky shore. [Note to author – maybe there should be a storm? Get a coast chart and find out the name of the island. It's on the satellite photos that are on the internet, but there is no name. Also, West End is the actual name of the city on St. Thomas, but will readers know that?]

The yacht is completely destroyed but everyone on board survives. The Coast Guard is looking in the wrong place because the Captain was so far off course; the Coast Guard will never find the survivors. The rescue effort is also hampered and then cancelled by a fast-moving tropical storm that quickly becomes a category two hurricane. The Coast Guard has more pressing business and is forced to protect those known to be alive instead of looking for those who may not be. When Brandon and Gail learn that the yacht is missing and the search has been abandoned, they mount their own rescue effort. Brandon is a licensed pilot and had served in the Air Force. Gail was driven by the fact that one of the bridesmaids had been her cousin.

No. Wally corrected the entry – not *had been – was*. She was still alive.

The Writer

Gail's father was once the skipper of a destroyer. He added his expertise to Brandon's and they worked out wind and current charts for the week before and after the charter boat went missing. Using that information, Brandon puts together a search pattern that starts at the last known position and moves in a step-wise manner down the path of the currents with minor adjustments for wind. But they don't know that the Captain was off course. Eventually they presume that he had to have been. Gail's father examines the charts and decides that the most likely navigational error would put the lost ship north of the Virgin Island, not south of them as the Coast Guard had presumed.

Brandon begins another search, finally finding the lost voyagers safe and sound on the island.

[Note to author – make up stories about what is happening on the island while the search is going on].

Walter looked at what he had written and he liked it. Kelly would be able to add all the detail necessary to turn the outline into a real story. Wally frowned. It was still missing something. Neither he nor Kelly had tried to live off the land after a shipwreck. Wally would just have to remedy that by scheduling more adventures for Kelly. He had read somewhere that some corporations send their employees on wilderness survival weekends in order to build camaraderie. That might be worth looking into.

The Writer

Walter Fleegle turned off his tablet and napped on the deck until dawn.

Wally had a stiff neck. He had really enjoyed sleeping on the deck, but as he stretched, he acknowledged that sleeping below in a soft bunk would have been a better idea. The sun was just coming up and the Captain had just rounded the point at the west end of St. Thomas. Wally could see the town of West End, but the harbor at Charlotte Amalie would be farther up ahead and off to port. Dead ahead, Wally could see Buck Island. The nature preserve in the shallows south of St. Thomas consisted of two islands, separated by a narrow and shallow pass. It was what the sailors called 'skinny water' and it was too shallow except at the very highest tides for a sailing ship with a keel to navigate. The rising sun seemed to be sitting in the notch between these two islands creating the impression that it had been set there to take a rest from its never-ending duty. The slot of the island formed the glow of the sun into rays that spread out sideways and upwards into a blue sky accented with wisps of pink clouds. The water between Wally and the islands was calm, but not flat, and glittered with the sparkles of dawn.

Spike stood in the bow pulpit looking ahead at the island. Wally thought that he should be smart enough to know not to look directly at the sun, and, at the moment, looking at the island meant looking at the sun. He was further surprised when Spike pulled out a pair of binoculars and glassed the area.

Putting the binoculars back into a pouch he carried at his side, Spike turned and trotted back towards the cockpit. "You're right, Skipper! There's a mast in the slot – and it's leaning hard over!"

90

The Writer

Wally heard Captain Jeffries mutter, "Some damn fool tried to shoot the cut during last night's high tide." The Captain adjusted his heading to make for the island instead of the harbor, adding his opinion of the navigational skills of the captain of the foundering ship up ahead. "Dumbass."

As Spike passed him making his way aft, Wally asked, "How can you tell the other boat is in trouble?"

Spike turned and pointed to the otherwise idyllic scene. "See the cant on that mast. It's supposed to be straight up. Leaning to the side like that can mean only one thing. Her keel is on the bottom. If she stays like that, the weight of the boat will drive her keel up through her bottom and tear her apart."

"Oh!" Wally said with sudden understanding.

Spike readied the skiff while the Captain engaged the motorized roller furling mechanism. The mainsail rolled up first, followed closely by the jib. While they were being hauled in, the diesel engines were started up. Once in gear, they added another six knots to the speed of the yacht. It didn't take long for the Captain to close the gap. When they got to within 500 yards, they could see people on the rocks waving for help. There isn't a standard set of horn signals in the navigation manual that means *We're coming to save you* so Captain Jeffries made something up. He gave one long blast indicating that he was approaching the channel. That was followed by five short blasts which is the signal for danger. Most of the passengers wouldn't know what he meant but hopefully a crewman was there who would. The passengers might interpret the horn as an acknowledgement that they had been seen. The crewman would know that he should ask people to

The Writer

be patient. The rescue ship didn't want to be the second vessel to run aground on the rocks that day.

The blasts on the horn not only alerted the people on the rocks that help was on the way, but they awakened Captain Jeffries' passengers. It wasn't long before the deck was cluttered with people who didn't know what to do. They were just in the way. It would be no use to ask them to return below and miss the excitement, so Spike got them al lined up and seated on top of the cabin.

Two hundred yards from shore, Captain Jeffries turned his yacht into the wind and put the engines in reverse. Spike let go the anchor and then raced to the stern to lower the skiff. The combination anchor rode (chain and then heavy line) rattled and then hummed as it was dragged through the hawse pipe by the weight of the big Danforth anchor. Wally could feel the ship shudder slightly as the anchor set itself and stopped the rearward movement of the vessel. At almost the exact same time, Spike loosened the lines that held the skiff on the davits, paying out bow and stern lines evenly, letting the blocks lower the small boat into the water.

"Get over there and get me a sitrep!" the Captain shouted to Spike as he unhooked the line from the lift-points and cranked the outboard to life. "Radio?" the Captain shouted as Spike passed up the starboard side. The mate just raised a hand holding the radio, showing the Captain that he had it with him.

Ten suspenseful minutes later, the radio crackled. "We've got 11 souls. Bumps and bruises. One possible broken arm."

"Copy that," the Captain replied. "Bring the broken arm back. Leave the rest. Give them the radio."

The Writer

While Spike brought the young lady with the broken arm back to the yacht, Captain Jeffries raised the harbor master at Charlotte Amalie. There was no immediate danger, so the Coast Guard deferred to the harbormaster, asking him to retrieve the passengers who were still on the island. They did, however, send out a small boat with a paramedic to look at the girl with the broken arm and bring her in to the hospital.

Captain Jeffries lay at anchor until the harbormaster's shuttle was able to get all the passengers off of the island. The biggest problem they had was not the rocks or the waves on the shore. The crew from the harbormaster's office had to convince the passengers that they were not going to be allowed to go back on board the foundered vessel and pack their belongings. It took a while, but they were eventually assured that the salvage company would return everything that they could.

The biggest problem that Captain Jeffries had was convincing his own passengers that he couldn't move closer without impeding the rescue. He apologized profusely for being anchored too far away for them to get good pictures with their cell phones.

Wally got out his tablet to make a note about the event, especially the whining: *Kelly needs a fancy camera and a big telephoto lens.* It was while he was doing that that he noticed the odd coincidence of having written a summary about a shipwreck and experiencing one only a few hours later.

Isn't that strange? he wrote. *Maybe there's a story in that?*

The Writer

CHAPTER ELEVEN

SCUBA CLASS

The harbor at Charlotte Amalie is quiet. But then again, harbors on small islands are supposed to be quiet. It's part of the whole island experience. Wally and the other passengers had the option of staying on the yacht or getting a room at the hotel just up the hill from the mooring. Wally wanted to see the town, but wasn't really interested in lugging his luggage around, so he picked up his tablet and walked out of the small harbor parking lot and across the street to a small row of shops. Spike had said that the passengers would be safe on the waterfront, but that they should be careful if they ventured up into town. There were areas that got pretty rough. Kelly wanted to venture up the hill further, but Wally talked him out of it. There were certain kinds of adventures that he didn't want Kelly to be able to write about from experience. Getting mugged, beaten up, or worse, were not the experiences he was seeking.

Wally found a small restaurant where he decided to have dinner later on. Along the way, he wandered through a few places that sold trinkets and local island products. The last little shop was a bar where he could get a drink. It had a small pool table and Walter assured Kelly that they would come back later. At the other end of the row of shops was a small dive shop. Wally went in and started to get interested in the underwater world. SCUBA diving

94

The Writer

was on his list of things that exciting people did, but he had assumed that he would need to take a six week course before going diving. The man in the shop told him a different story.

"We have something called a Resort Course," the young man explained. "We can take anyone, even if they can't swim, and give them the SCUBA experience. We start with an hour of lecture where we teach you the most important things and then we show you all the gear. That takes about an hour too. After that, we get on the boat and put to sea!"

"Isn't that dangerous?" Walter asked, somewhat nervously.

"Not at all!" the man replied. "We pair students with instructors one-on-one. All you need to do is what you're told to do. Now, you don't end up with a certification, but you do get three hours of diving. You can even rent a camera! Of course our own photographers will be taking stills and video of the entire experience. Prints and DVDs will be available after the dive."

Wally picked up the little flier that was on the counter. It was all there in black and white. *Not really*, Wally corrected himself. It was a full color, heavy-stock, glossy promotional piece, covered front and back with all the wonders of the sea and testimonials to how great the experience was. In smaller print, Wally found the details. Eight AM to noon – training. Noon to five PM – diving. Five to ten – dinner and drinks on the house.

"That looks good." Kelly interrupted.

"It's $800.00," Wally pointed out.

"I need something cool to write about," Kelly persisted.

"Can't we rent some old movies? *The Deep* should be pretty cheap by now," Wally objected.

The Writer

"Do you want to do this or not?" Kelly prodded.

"Do what?" Wally mused. "The writing or the diving?"

"Both," Kelly replied. "You need to do one if you want me to do the other."

Wally caved. "In for a penny, in for a pound."

"Oh!" Kelly scoffed. "That's original! Can I use that?"

"Shut up," Wally ordered. "We're doin' it."

Walter made the arrangements for the resort course, thanked the man and wandered back outside to try to find something to eat. At a little open-air café a few shops down, he settled into a chair and turned on his laptop. "What are you doing?" Kelly asked.

"I'm going to do a test," Wally replied.

"Go on." Kelly wanted to know more.

"I know you already know the rest." Wally was getting overwhelmed by Kelly's nagging. But then, he accepted the fact that Kelly was helping him to resolve his uncertainties by forcing him to think about them. "I'm going to write a story about the dive trip tomorrow." Wally almost sneered at Kelly. "Then, after we get back, you can write one and we'll compare them. That way I can see what effect our excursions are having on our writing."

"I see." Kelly mused. "Actually, that's not a bad idea."

Wally readied himself at the tablet but was interrupted by the waitress.

"Did you want something?" she asked.

The Writer

Remembering that he had come to the café because he was hungry, Wally ordered a Pita pocket sandwich with turkey and cheese.

"Tea?" the waitress asked. "Beer? Water?"

"I'll have a tea, please," Wally responded. He was relieved when she left. Maybe now, he thought, he could begin his story.

Diving - by Walter Fleegle

Summary: A story about a man who takes a resort course from a dive shop in the Virgin Islands.

Kent Clarkson …

"Kent Clarkson?" Kelly laughed. "That's original!"

"Leave me alone," Wally ordered. "If you interrupt, I can't do this."

Walter started over.

Kent Clarkson was big, strong, tall, and handsome. He had black hair and wore black rimmed glasses. He was on vacation in the Virgin Islands and decided to learn how to SCUBA dive. His friend, a Mr. Bland Kelton, would not be going with him. Bland had been aptly named. He had no character. He had no charisma. None of his features were worth taking notice of.

The Writer

"That pretty much sucks," Kelly interrupted.

"Shut up," Wally said. "I'm just laying the groundwork. I'll punch it up later."

"I meant the part about calling me bland," Kelly said.

"Shut up!" Wally screamed at Kelly. "If you don't behave, we're not going!"

Kelly didn't answer, so Walter continued his story.

On the morning of the dive, Kent went to the dive shop and suffered through a three hour lecture. He told himself that he was cool and tough. He didn't need a lecture. Kent just wanted to put the equipment on and get in the water. He tried to pay attention but was distracted by some of the other people in the class. Apparently, there was a college cheerleading squad on vacation too. There were six of them. They were all going on the dive trip with him. There was only one other man in the group of eight students. He was a nerdy guy. He was small and skinny.

When the lecture was over, Kent went back to his room and put on his swim suit. He got a jacket like the instructor said and went back to the boat. The girls were already there. Kent stared at the long legs that started at flip-flops and ended in six perfectly rounded asses that were inadequately covered by skimpy bikinis. They all wore their jackets so he

The Writer

couldn't check out their tits. Kent consoled himself because he knew those jackets were coming off later. Kent was a very curious person. He wondered if those asses were tight and round because of the cheerleading workouts or if the tight round asses were what got the girls onto the squad in the first place.

Kent got on the boat and was surprised by how it rocked. He helped each cheerleader get from the dock to the boat, but left the nerdy guy to get on by himself. That was when the captain and the instructors arrived.

The captain smiled. "You were supposed to wait for us to get on. You could get hurt."

Kent grinned. He never got hurt. He was cool and tough.

The captain started talking about safety again. He said something about life jackets. That was all Kent remembered hearing. He was smiling across the deck at the tall blonde cheerleader and admiring the fit of her bikini. She smiled back at him. He thought that he would probably fuck her first. Kent was handsome and attractive and he knew it. He was handsome enough that he could have almost any girl he wanted. He wanted the tall blonde.

"Really?" Kelly interrupted again. "Is this a story about a dive trip or a romance novel? Maybe you're preparing something for a letter to a girly magazine!"

The Writer

"Shut up!" Wally replied. "I'm trying to give the story some meat!"

"It sounds like you're trying to give the cheerleader Kent's meat," Kelly joked.

"Oh, jeez," Wally said in exasperation.

"Okay, okay," Kelly said. "Go on. I can't wait to see how this experiment turns out."

Wally continued.

The captain untied the boat and turned the engines on. Soon they were in the harbor and then soon after that they were near a small island about three miles south of the harbor. The captain dropped the anchor and the instructors began to pair up with the students. Each instructor helped their student put on the equipment. Kent was right about getting to check out the girls' tits. He watched eagerly as each of the girls took off her jacket and put on the SCUBA tanks. After leering at them all, he confirmed his earlier supposition. He would fuck the tall blonde girl first.

The instructors got everyone ready and then each of them jumped into the water off of the back end of the boat. Kent laughed because the nerdy guy didn't do it right and his mask came off. He looked pretty scared but the instructor got his mask and put it back on. For $800.00 the instructor wasn't going to let a little thing like a dislodged mask ruin the day.

The Writer

Underwater Kent saw lots of brightly colored fish, a sea turtle, and a big grouper. The bottom was rocky and had corals and seaweed growing on it. It was very colorful and a lot of fun. The instructors took them to a sandy place on the bottom and told them to kneel in the sand. Each of them posed for the camera. That was when Kent made his first move on the blonde girl. He motioned to her that she should come kneel beside him for a picture. She did, of course. He knew she would. Kent was cool and handsome. What he didn't know was that she had picked him out too. She had decided that he would be her first pick. Of course his competition was the nerdy guy – but there were eight instructors too.

After a couple of pictures with the blonde girl, the other five cheerleaders all came over too. Kent positioned himself with three cheerleaders on each side and smiled for the camera.

After they had their picture taken, the instructors spread them out again on the sand. Each instructor gave each diver a small piece of fish. They waved the fish – or maybe it was crab meat – in the water and the colorful little reef fish came to them. The little reef fish ate right out of their hands.

The dive was over and the instructors started taking the divers back to the boat. When they were all back on board, the captain started the engines. Someone pulled up the anchor and they went back to

101

The Writer

the dock for the dinner and drinks as promised in the promotion.

"Are you gonna write about how Kent makes his move on blondie and fucks her?" Kelly interrupted.

"I thought I'd try," Wally said.

"Forget it." Kelly dismissed Wally's thought.

"You're right," Wally admitted. He wouldn't know where to begin. And he certainly wouldn't be able to write about how the blonde girl had decided to fuck Kent. That would be too bizarre. It would be a good story though if Kent ended up working his way through the entire squad. Wally quickly rejected the idea. He wasn't going to be that kind of writer.

"I could write about the hot dogs and beer." Wally consoled himself. "I've eaten hot dogs before."

"Forget it," Kelly said. "There's no story in a hot dog." He then retracted his statement. "Well, unless the hot dog is poison, or maybe laced with roofies so that Kent can get blondie into bed. Or maybe the hot dog has tiny electronic tracking devices in it because Kent is really a spy and the bad spies want to keep track of him? You could make blondie a Russian spy!"

"Maybe," Wally said. "Or maybe I'll have the cheerleaders forget about Kent and have *all* of them go fuck the nerdy guy. You know? Out of pity? At least I know about that!"

"True." Kelly conceded the point. "But why does anybody need to fuck or get fucked? Can't a story be a good story without everybody getting horizontal?"

The Writer

"Sex sells," Wally said flatly and with authority. "It said so in the writer's manual. Anyway, this is my story. You get your chance tomorrow."

"And another thing," Kelly added, "why use the fuck word? What about intercourse, carnal relations, love-making, and melding of the souls?"

"Because, dumbass," Wally explained. "When it's just humping, there's no love or soul-melding involved. It's just pure hedonistic fucking: fucking for personal pleasure not for the pleasure of the partner or for making babies. That's the difference between fucking and love-making."

"How do you know that?" Kelly asked.

"I'm guessing." Walter lied somewhat sadly. "Now let's go get a room at the hotel. I need a nap."

"Really?" Kelly asked.

"Yeah," Wally replied turning off the tablet. "You wear me out."

Wally paid for his sandwich and asked the waitress for a to-go box. "Sorry," he explained. "I got distracted. I'm sure it's good. I'll eat it later."

She said that he didn't need to explain, smiled, and packed it up for him.

In the hotel room, Walter ate his sandwich and turned on the tablet again. "Hey dumbass," Kelly said. "You forgot to save your little story, didn't you?"

"DAMN!" Wally cursed.

The Writer

"I bet you never even turned on the auto-save feature, did you?" Kelly continued to be a prick.

Wally looked. There was a f le remnant. He opened it, anticipating the best. He found the worst. The auto-save had been set for 15 minutes and the saved portion of his story ended just before he had started writing about the others in the class. There were no cheerleaders. There was no nerdy guy.

"It doesn't really matter," Kelly teased. "It was a decent story line, but the writing sucked. You had short sentences and run-on sentences. Most of it was choppy and on more than one occasion, you started several sentences in a row with the same noun or pronoun. And, by the way, *Captain* should be capitalized."

"Damn," Walter cursed more calmly. Flopping into the bed, he shut down the tablet and turned on the television.

Walter Fleegle was in a funk all night. He wanted to try to rewrite his story, but it was gone. All night long he dreamed of colorful little fish and tight little cheerleaders.

In the morning, though, he did feel better. Coffee, a bagel, and a small bowl of fruit from the complimentary breakfast bar put him in a downright up-minded mood. Today he was going diving.

"No." Kelly rejected Wally's happy thought. "Today I'm going diving. Remember the experiment?"

Wally knew that he could exercise his right to be the only person in his head any time that he wanted to, but the truth was that he didn't want to; at least not yet. Inventing Kelly had been internally divisive, but it had allowed a side of Wally to emerge that Wally was enjoying – even if Kelly was a jackass from time to time.

"You're right," Wally admitted. "You're going diving."

The Writer

The change in Wally was becoming more distinct and more easily accomplished every time that he let Kelly take over. Kelly was developing the kind of self-assured attitude that had eluded Walter for his entire life. Kelly needed to go diving.

Kelly put on his swimming trunks and looked at himself in the mirror. He thought he looked good. He was trim, if not muscular. Wally kept telling Kelly that the active lifestyle that he had adopted had seemed to add a little muscle to his frame, but Kelly wasn't happy. He wanted to spend time at the gym and get some definition. He wanted to be physically confident as well. That damn short leg was holding him back. In a somewhat feeble attempt to compensate, Kelly had gone out and purchased special flip-flops. They were custom made and were expensive, but the half inch thicker sole on the thong for his short leg made his hips even when he stood still. He could actually stand straight and tall without looking off-balance.

Smiling, Kelly put on a shirt and a pair of shorts over his suit, picked up his notebook and went off to seek adventure at the dive shop. The walk from the hotel to the shop was not long, and while Kelly thought that Wally's story was pretty crappy, he did enjoy the speculation that there might be girls in the class. When he opened the dive shop door and saw six women in their fifties his hope was destroyed.

There were no slender legs, no tight asses, and no perky boobs. The Dayton, Ohio, bridge club had won a trip to the Virgin Islands. Only six of the forty-seven members had been able to take advantage of the prize. It was Kelly's grand luck to have chosen the same day as they had for their first foray beneath the waves. Kelly smiled pleasantly at the six overweight women and took a seat at

The Writer

the table. Unlike the characters in Wally's story, Kelly thought that nobody in this class was having lustful thoughts.

The instructors began instructing and Kelly did his best to pay attention. He was keenly aware of the fact that people don't normally live under water. Using the equipment properly was the one thing that would keep him, and the others, alive.

Twenty minutes into the training, the class was interrupted. Giselle opened the door to the classroom as quietly as she could and slipped into the seat beside Kelly. He had only wondered about the eighth student in passing up until that time. When Giselle sat next to him, he was thankful.

Giselle was not exceptionally pretty, but, he thought, she did smell nice. She was average height, for a woman, and like most women in their mid-thirties, she carried a few extra pounds. Kelly smiled at her and when she smiled back there was a little light behind her eyes that made him like her. Her hair was dark, almost black, but not quite. Right above her widow's peak was a streak of pure white hair that gave her a whimsical and playful look. She looked at the notes he had taken and tried to catch up with the rest of the class.

The rest of the morning was uneventful, but Kelly did learn a lot about partial gas pressures, the properties of gasses that were dissolved in a liquid – like air in a person's blood – and about thermal physics. The instructor made a strong point of making sure that everyone had to bring a jacket.

"But it's 87 degrees outside," one bridge player objected.

"And you told us that the water was 89!" another added.

The Writer

"That's right," the instructor explained. "But your body is 98.6 degrees and water takes away heat twenty-five times faster than air. You'll probably feel fine while you're in the water even though you will be losing body heat rapidly. It's after you get out that you might feel cold; especially since we are going to be out late in the day. If we get any cloud cover at all, I can almost guarantee that you will be cold.

It wasn't until the instructor ended class, telling the students to get some lunch and meet at the boat later, that Kelly had a chance to introduce himself to Giselle.

"Hello." He smiled a now well-practiced crooked smile. "I'm Kelly. Kelly Blanton."

Giselle smiled her sparkly smile again. "Nice to meet you. I'm Giselle Winkler. I hope I didn't interrupt the class too much. I'm sorry I was late."

"Stop apologizing!" Kelly admonished her. "You're fine. If you have lunch with me, I'll fill you in on what you missed."

"Shouldn't the instructors do that?" Giselle asked.

"I'm sure they would if you asked them," Kelly replied.

Giselle smiled again. "I think you're probably the kind of man who takes good notes."

Wally interrupted – or, rather, he tried. "What are you doing?

Kelly ignored him as he assessed his situation. Giselle was friendly and apparently alone. The confident self-assured man that Wally was trying to bring out in Kelly would certainly strike up a friendship, even if it was to be limited to the next eight hours. If

The Writer

Giselle had not joined the group, Kelly would have befriended the bridge club – but with different expectations.

It wasn't until they got to the small café a few doors down from the dive shop that Kelly noticed that Giselle did not wear a wedding ring. Over lunch, he learned that she was from New Jersey. She owned a small farm in Warren County, where she raised some livestock and made cheese from milk she bought from her neighbors. The sad part of her story was that she had inherited the land when her husband had passed away in a tragic accident. Her two children had long ago moved away. One was in Texas and the other in Utah. One day, she decided that she was lonely and the next thing she knew she was on a plane for St. Thomas.

"I'm sort of spontaneous like that," she explained and smiled again.

"How'd you get here?" she asked.

"You better not tell!" Wally njected.

"Well," Kelly explained. "It's sort of the same story as you. One day I realized that I needed a little more adventure in my life so I bought a plane ticket."

"What do you do? For a living, I mean," Giselle persisted.

"Don't tell!" Wally objected.

"It's a good sign when a woman wants to know more about you," Kelly said to Wally so that Giselle couldn't hear.

Kelly suppressed Wally's interruption and smiled at Giselle. "I'm sort of a money-changer."

"You mean like in the Bible?" Giselle asked astounded. "Like a banker or something?"

The Writer

"No." Kelly shook his head and took a big chance. "I collect tolls. I sit in a booth next to the highway all day, collect money and give people change." Giselle looked a little surprised. Kelly continued. "But, remember when I said that I needed some more excitement?" Giselle nodded. "Well, when I realized that, I started to make changes. First I decided that I wanted to pursue my first career choice – writing. Then I decided to go nuts. Since then, I've taken skydiving lessons and flying lessons and now today, SCUBA diving lessons! I even got shooting lessons and bought a handgun."

Kelly went for broke and Wally went nuts. "But in all that, the most exciting thing so far has been meeting you."

Giselle blushed. "That's sweet, but I doubt that it's true."

"No. Really!" Kelly persisted.

"How's that?" Giselle had not expected him to continue with what she considered to be a transparent charade.

"Those other things?" Kelly paused to enhance the suspense. "I knew what to expect. I knew that when I jumped out of the airplane, the chute would open and I would float to the ground. The gun I bought has a manual." Kelly grinned. "With you, everything is uncertain. I could have a soft landing or crash at 600 miles an hour." Kelly went so far as to give Giselle a wink as he asked, "You don't come with operating instructions, do you?"

Giselle blushed again. "No." She shook her head. "I don't."

"I can't believe you!" Wally exclaimed.

"Shut up," Kelly replied.

The Writer

"So, you decided to be a writer?" Giselle asked. "Were you going to write a set of operating instructions for me?" She blushed again. "Am I going to be a chapter in your book?"

Kelly smiled his crooked smile. "Let's wait to see if there's anything to write about, shall we?" He waved to the waitress for the check. "We should get going."

"Un fucking believable!" Wally screamed. "She bought that shit?"

"Of course not." Kelly tried to calm Wally down. "She's flirting. I'm flirting. We both know it's bullshit, but it's good bullshit."

Giselle excused herself after Kelly paid the waitress. She had to go to her room to change. Kelly did too, but sensed that Giselle needed a little time to herself. How he knew that, he couldn't tell. Neither he nor Wally were experienced in these matters. He and Wally agreed this newfound sense could only have arisen from the newfound self-confidence. Kelly gave Giselle a two-minute head start before he went back to the hotel to get his jacket.

Kelly arrived at the boat to find that the bridge club had already gathered and was waiting for the Captain. Giselle had not yet arrived.

"I wonder if being late is a thing with her." Kelly mused.

"Where's Giselle?" the Captain asked as he arrived and counted students.

"She'll be here soon," Kelly responded. "She went to get something from her room."

The Writer

A parade of instructors had followed the Captain down the dock and soon the entire group had gathered — everyone except Giselle.

"You scared her off, you asshole," Wally muttered.

"No. I didn't," Kelly replied as Giselle came around the corner of the harbormaster's office and strutted towards the boat, her smile locked onto Kelly.

"Come on!" Kelly called to her. "You're holding up the whole adventure!"

Giselle laughed and so did the bridge club. She tossed her bag to a waiting instructor and attempted to negotiate the two-foot gap between the side of the boat and the dock. Stepping down onto the boat from the dock, Kelly noticed that she was unsteady. Taking advantage of her momentary loss of balance, he held his hand up to her. She took it and smiled at him, once again lighting him up with the sparkle in her eyes.

The Captain pressed the starter button and the two outboard engines sputtered to life.

"Cast off all lines!"

Two of the instructors let go of the mooring lines, fore and aft. Each of them shoved against the dock and the dive boat floated free. When it had drifted about three feet, the Captain put her in gear and they motored casually out to the dive site.

Kelly would have liked to have had time to engage in more flirting with Giselle, but the time was needed to get their gear prepared and fitted. Each one had to have the straps adjusted so that their tanks didn't flop around. Kelly thought it amusing that

The Writer

the instructors had to take his straps in while letting them out for the bridge club.

Seated on the bench seat that ran along the side of the boat, Kelly watched the instructor adjust Giselle's straps. Everything about her was in sharp contrast to the ladies in the club. While she was not in the same class as the blonde that Wally had imagined yesterday, she was quite attractive. She had not chosen a bikini, but instead wore a flattering one piece suit. It was all black, which only served to accentuate both her hair and the white streak in it. Her figure was well proportioned. Both Wally and Kelly found it pleasing. More than that, they realized that Giselle herself was pleasing.

With each instructor fitting gear onto each student, making sure that they knew how to use it, turning air on, applying defogging soap to the masks, and everything else that was necessary to get ready for a dive, there was little time for Kelly and Giselle to interact. During the dive itself, of course, there were even fewer opportunities. The two had to settle for an occasional glance, a smile, or a wink to let each other know that they were interested.

The dive itself was remarkable. Kelly was fascinated by the corals, sea fans, streamers of algae, and the fish. What surprised him the most was how many different kinds of corals he spotted. Some were like plates, growing on the rock and taking the shape of it just like plates or clocks in a Dali painting. Others stuck up into the water almost like trees. One was like a pile of sticks: long pieces of coral in a jumble that sat on top of the rock beneath. Growing among these colorful and calm animals Kelly saw sea fans, sea whips, and a myriad of sponges. The fans looked just like the name implied. They were flat and wide, stuck to the bottom at one end while the fan floated back and forth in the water with each wave

The Writer

that passed overhead. The sea whips were like soft pieces of … hmmm … *what was the word Kelly needed*? He had it. They were like long skinny sausages. They were firm, but not solid.

The sponges came in all different shapes and sizes. Some were like bowls, some like vases that one might fill with flowers. Others were flat and coated the surface of the rock like spilled paint. Many were tubular and growing together in a clump, making them look like a pile of rope. The one Kelly liked the most was a barrel-shaped sponge. It was hollow inside and was a little larger than a five gallon bucket.

Kelly spent a long time admiring one of the barrel-like sponges growing at the base of a pile of rocks. It had attached itself right above where the rocks met the sandy bottom that surrounded them. Glancing up, he noticed Giselle on the other side of the small rock outcrop. She was watching a sea turtle that had swum into the midst of the divers. Apparently this particular turtle had seen enough divers to know that it didn't need to be afraid of them. They were both startled when the turtle glided casually over to the barrel sponge and took a large bite out of it.

Looking to his right, Kelly saw the bridge club kneeling in the sand. The photographer was taking a group photograph. When the flash stopped going off, an instructor started passing out scraps of fish. The ladies all held their piece of fish out in front of them as they had been told to do. It didn't take long before hundreds of small fish were swirling in the water, darting in to take a bite out of their offering. The photographer was taking pictures like mad. Kelly wondered how much he would get for each print.

The Writer

At least Wally had gotten that part of the story right. But then again, the promotional piece did have pictures of that as part of the experience.

A few minutes after the feeding started, a large shark drifted by over the heads of the bridge club. Kelly and Giselle could see it, but the ladies never knew it was there. After a while, one of the ladies started to get cold, just as the instructor had predicted. When she shivered, her instructor asked if she wanted to go up by giving her a thumbs-up signal. Everywhere else in the world, this hand signal means that you are okay. Not underwater. She nodded and the two started their ascent to the boat. That scene repeated itself at irregular intervals five more times over the next twenty minutes, eventually leaving Kelly, Giselle, and their two instructors as the hold-outs.

Giselle found a sea urchin and picked it up, letting it grab onto her hand with its thousands of tiny sucker-like feet. When she saw Kelly watching her, she swam over to him and they both studied the movement of the spines and the little feet. At one point they marveled at how it had ejected something from a small disk-like thing on its back. *Well, it didn't really have a back*, Kelly told himself. *It was the top.*

Kelly was enthralled with the small fish that seemed to be everywhere. The wrasses, grunts, snappers, blennies, and gobies swam, darted, hid, and even crawled around the reef. Of course there were shrimp, crabs, and snails in abundance too, but it was the fish that captured Kelly's attention.

That and the way Giselle seemed to be so graceful in the water. He made a mental note to be sure to compliment her on that during dinner.

The Writer

The dive was over much too soon to suit Kelly. Apparently Giselle had felt the same way because her instructor had to practically drag her back to the surface. By the time Kelly and Giselle got back on board, the ladies in the bridge club had already removed their equipment, dried off, donned their jackets, and were baking in the sun to rewarm themselves. The instructor was right about the feeling of being cold. Both he and Giselle had goose bumps.

During the ride back to shore, Giselle had found a seat on the bench on the starboard side of the boat and Kelly sat on the port side. As luck had it, they were facing each other, dying to talk about their experience, but the noise of the outboards was too great. They would have to wait until later.

"I'm hungry," Kelly said after the Captain shut down the engines at the dock.

"Me too," Giselle replied. "I'm going to take a shower and wash the salt out of my hair. I'll see you later? The excursion includes dinner and drinks, you know."

Kelly smiled at the thought that she would want him there. "I'll be there."

Wally waited until Kelly was out of the shower before he started asking Kelly what he would write. "Okay! Now that you've been diving, let's see what you got!"

Kelly rejected the idea. "The day's not over yet."

"The dive is!" Wally countered. "The bet was about writing about the dive."

Kelly had to admit that Wally was right. The bad part about being a voluntary schizophrenic is that you can't lie to yourself. You

The Writer

can be in denial and even delusional, but you always know when you're telling yourself out-and-out lies.

Wally handed the tablet to Kelly. "Go."

The Dive - by Kelly Blanton

Summary: Kent Clarkson, the ruggedly handsome construction worker from Nevada was tired of being a slave to his job. When the opportunity arose one day to take a week-long trip to the US Virgin Islands and learn to SCUBA dive, he jumped at it. As soon as he saw the advertisement for the trip, he realized that he had become so committed to his job in order to cover the pain of being alone. His beautiful young wife of only three years had died 18 months ago. Both she and the baby she carried were taken from him at the same time. Even though he knew he wasn't responsible, he blamed himself. He could've gotten a better doctor for the delivery. He could've gone to a better hospital for the C-section that the doctor claimed was necessary. There were so many things that he could've done, none of which would have actually changed the outcome, but all of which weighed heavily on him. His only solace was the distraction that building new homes gave him. When he wasn't working, he volunteered at the urban home project that built and gave away new homes to needy families. This trip to the islands would be his release.

The Writer

In St. Thomas, he found a dive shop that taught the quickie course. It was expensive, but Kent didn't care. He wanted to be free from the guilt and free from the burial ground of construction work. He was in luck. Among the people in his dive class was a young woman named Lucy. She too had lost her husband and she too was looking for solace. It was a dangerous combination. They were two lonely people carrying an undeserved burden who suddenly found themselves in a tropical paradise engaged in all the new underwater experiences that thrilled the soul and warmed the heart. Circumstances conspired to keep them somewhat separated during the day, but they still found time to flirt with nothing more than a glance or a smile. By the end of the day, with their endorphins rocketing into overdrive, they finally found time to be together for drinks and dinner. There could be only one outcome.

"Are you kidding me?" Wally interrupted. "Is Kent gonna fuck Lucy?"

"Maybe Lucy's the horny aggressive one," Kelly replied. "I haven't got there yet."

"Maybe you're the horny one!" Wally shot back. "Are you gonna make a move on Giselle tonight?"

"Why shouldn't I?" Kelly asked.

"Why should you?" Wally countered.

The Writer

"She clearly likes me," Kelly replied with a smug grin.

"She doesn't even know you. Hell you're not even real," Wally grunted at Kelly.

"Doesn't matter," Kelly parried. "She wants me."

"You don't know that." Wally groaned. "And what about what you said about fucking? This isn't a story, now. This is real life. If you fuck Giselle, then you're scum. You're hedonistic, uncaring scum."

"What if I make love to her?" Kelly asked.

"You can't!" Wally cried. "You don't love her!"

Kelly considered his position. "What if she fucks me? What if she's the horny, hedonistic scum? Should I let her have me? You know that I'm going to need to have that experience eventually if you want me to write about it."

Damn. Wally thought. *He's using my own argument against me.*

"If you let her do that, then you'll only be hurting her in the long run. You know that stuff never works out. If she's that horny then it's not because she needs a romp, it's because she misses the friendship and companionship of her husband." Wally put his foot down. "No. You can't fuck her even if she wants it. Even if she begs you!"

"She'll just go get it somewhere else," Kelly said. "You know she will."

Kelly's point was hard to argue with. Wally picked up the tablet and finished Kelly's summary.

The Writer

Lucy's eyes were damp. Through the tears, Kent was even more attractive than he had been out on the reef. She had been right about him. He was not just handsome. He had a soul and apparently his soul had found its way into hers. Somehow he knew that she was still suffering the loss of her husband. Somehow he knew that she was desperate for a man. Somehow he knew that she needed a companion more than she needed an orgasm. When she had suggested that they go up to her room, Kent had calmly taken her hand and explained that they could do that, but that it would be empty and hollow. He told her that by morning, when she was to get on a plane that would take her home, she would regret it.

"You've broken out of the trance that your loss created," Kent told her. "This trip is the first step to regain control of your life, not the last one in a life that you can think of with self-respect. You need to go home and find a man who can be a partner and not just partner with some random man."

Wally hit the save button and turned off the tablet.

Kelly caught up with Giselle on the patio behind the dive shop just as the instructors were taking the hot dogs and hamburgers off the grill.

"Hi!" She smiled and reached out to take his hand.

The Writer

Kelly took her hand and gave it a friendly squeeze. "How did you like that?"

"The dive?" She grinned. "Or the touch of your hand?"

"I need a beer," Kelly said. "Where's the cooler?"

Giselle was somewhat taken aback by Kelly's unusual response, but she hid it.

"It's over there. Come on. I'll show you."

Kelly got a beer and the two of them made their way through the line to get their dinner. Picking out a table that was off to the side, they were able to avoid the boisterous bridge club.

Giselle took Kelly's hand again, smiled her sparkly smile, and asked, "Did I do something wrong?"

"What do you mean?" Kelly asked.

"We're both grownups," she replied. "I'm not going to lie or play games. Unless I'm really confused, we've been flirting with each other since you let me look at your notes in class this morning."

Kelly nodded in agreement.

"I had thought …" she started, then corrected herself. "No. I had hoped that you and I would end up together this evening."

"We're together," Kelly said.

"I mean together as in upstairs in my room – or your room – and naked together." She smiled and squeezed his hand. "Is that a better picture of what I had in mind?"

Kelly couldn't believe what he was saying. He was unable to stop himself. "It wouldn't be right," he explained. "It would be fun

The Writer

and I would really, truly, like to see you naked and do ... naked stuff." Kelly put his other hand on top of Giselle's and continued his explanation. "But the truth is that you deserve more than ... naked stuff ... with some guy you just met. You're a really special person. I can see that. I don't know how, but I can just feel it. What you are suggesting is, frankly, beneath you."

"I'd rather be beneath you." Giselle played off of his words, hoping to change his mind.

"For a while, maybe," Kelly replied. "But what about next week? How would you feel then?" Kelly squeezed her hands and saw her eyes start to glisten. "You've lost something recently; lost someone recently. Don't lose your self-respect too. You don't need someone to stir up things that you can't put away. You need someone to stir up your heart. You need to go home, but don't go back to your isolation."

"We'll never see each other again, will we?" Giselle asked.

"Probably not," Kelly replied, "but I'll always remember you."

"Am I gonna be a chapter in your book?" she asked.

"If you are, it'll be one that you can show to your friends without blushing," Kelly said. "Now let's eat."

"Nicely done!" Wally exclaimed.

"Where the shit did all that come from?" Kelly asked Wally.

Startled by the question, Wally's mind raced back to the tablet. "I wrote it," he admitted. "I finished your summary while you weren't looking. I hit save."

"Can you erase it and rewrite it?" Kelly asked. "I'd really like to fuck her. And she really did want me to."

121

The Writer

"Not anymore she doesn't," Wally said. "Look at her. She doesn't want to take you upstairs. Now she wants to take you home."

Kelly looked at Giselle and smiled. Wally was right. She smiled back, but this time the look was different. It wasn't a flirty smile. It was a sad smile of loss combined with the happiness of being back on track. She wasn't going to spin off into a world of self-gratification and hide from her sorrow. She was going to conquer it. But she would have to do so without the man who had saved her.

"What you said, what you did, and what you didn't do struck a chord with her," Wally continued.

The moment was interrupted by the instructors as they began passing out certificates proving that the students had taken the abbreviated course and gone on their dive. That was immediately followed by a rather intense marketing effort by the photographers. Wally smiled as he watched Giselle purchase a photograph of herself and another of Kelly.

The Writer

CHAPTER TWELVE

HANG GLIDING

"What do you want to do now?" Wally asked Kelly over morning coffee.

"We can go horse-back riding over on St. John," Kelly suggested, "or we can go hang gliding off the cliff at Red Hook on the east end."

"We can ride a horse back home." Wally decided. "Let's go hang gliding. It'll give you something to write about."

"Hey!" Kelly asked. "Who won the writing bet from yesterday?"

"You did," Wally admitted. "My story sucked. Your summary was halfway decent, even if you never did get it into an actual story."

"So that proves our theory. Write about what you know about. I wrote about the diving because I'd gone diving. You finished my summary with what you know about."

"What do you mean?" Wally was uncertain where Kelly was going.

"You know about figuring out the right thing to do." Kelly appeased Wally and soothed his ego at the same time.

The Writer

"What I don't get is why I told Giselle what I told her," Kelly mused. "You were nowhere to be found and all that shit just came out of my mouth."

"We have the same morals," Wally explained. "You can't break them without us becoming truly schizophrenic instead of this experimental schizophrenia that we have."

"Good point," Kelly admitted. "But that means that you can write as well as I can write. We have the same imagination. And as I have an experience, even though I'm the one having it, you will be able to write about it too. That's the theory right?"

Wally nodded. "You bring self-confidence. If I ever develop that, I won't need you anymore." Wally thought for a moment, then added, "But I'd still use the pen name Kelly Blanton. It's a better name."

"Thank you, Wally." Kelly was appreciative of the sentiment.

"You're quite welcome. Now let's see if you're right." Wally tossed out an idea. "Let's see if I can draw on your imagination and write a better story about-hang gliding than I did about diving."

"Okay." Kelly laughed. "This should be fun. Are you going to write the whole story or just the summary?"

"Let's start with the summary. Let's see if I can get a plot together before I try and write it all out," Wally suggested.

"What do we need?" Kelly asked.

"We need characters, of course. And we need excitement – maybe some drama." Wally began to make a mental list.

"Sex?" Kelly asked. "It was you who said that sex sells."

The Writer

"I think we can leave that out for today," Wally said. "We almost got into trouble with that yesterday and I don't want to repeat that experience any time soon."

"Yeah," Kelly replied. "Almost getting laid is a hell of a lot worse than not having the chance at all."

"Can we move on?" Wally turned on the tablet and began his summary.

Hang It All - by Walter Fleegle

"Where do you get these goofy titles?" Kelly interrupted.

"Working here!" Wally replied and kept typing.

Summary: Kelly Blanton had always been afraid of heights. Recently, though, he had determined that he would conquer his fears one by one and become a better man. He had already taken flying lessons and had parachuted from an airplane. Today he would jump off of a cliff and fly like a kite. Of course, he would have an instructor, just as he had with his previous two challenges to his fear. If he could force himself to do it, he felt that he could declare himself the winner.

Kelly found the hang gliding shop located at the bottom of the steep cliff that would be their takeoff point. The day was early, but there were already two

The Writer

gliders floating 500 feet over the Caribbean. They looked peaceful as they made long lazy circles in the sky. Kelly went inside, made the arrangements, and was soon in a van being driven to the top of the cliff. The van parked in a large grassy area where three other gliders were putting the frame of their flying machines together and attaching the fabric to the wings. His instructor did the same, after which he helped Kelly put on his harness. Just as he had been during his skydiving experience, he would be attached to the instructor's harness. Today, for the introductory lesson, he would be a passenger. He wasn't even allowed to run and jump off the cliff. The instructor had Kelly hold his feet up off the ground while the instructor ran off the edge and into the air.

Peace. That's what Kelly felt. He wasn't afraid at all. He was completely at ease. It was quiet, comfortable, and peaceful. Kelly Blanton had won. Fear had lost.

"Are you gonna put any drama in this at all or what?" Kelly interrupted.

"I could make you crash into the sea," Wally suggested.

"Well," Kelly rejected the idea, "it doesn't have to be about me. I just wanted to see if you could add some drama."

Wally nodded. It would be good practice to try something along those lines. "Okay. Here goes."

The Writer

Kelly was enjoying his ride on the thermal that rose up off of the water. The altimeter that he had been given told him that he was floating as free as a bird at 1,100 feet. That's when his calm enjoyment was shattered by the scream of a woman. Snapping his head towards the sound, Kelly saw a hang glider in trouble: a lot of trouble. Part of the fabric of her wing had torn. She wasn't plummeting to the earth, but she was going down and she was going fast. Kelly wasn't really sure how these things worked, but he could tell that while she seemed to have some control, she had lost the ability to stay aloft. The woman narrowly avoided crashing into the side of the cliff, an event that would probably have destroyed the rest of her glider and sent her to her death. Falling fast, she aimed her glider off shore away from the rocks. A second glider chased after her. Kelly could tell that it was an instructor because the students all had multi-colored wings and the instructors all flew gliders with red wings.

"Do you need that much detail in the summary?" Kelly asked.

"Being able to tell who's who is important in this bit of drama that you wanted," Wally replied and kept typing.

The Writer

The instructor had put himself in a steep, yet controlled dive and was actually catching up with the woman. After what seemed like an incredibly long time to Kelly and microseconds to the woman in distress, she managed to flare a bit just before hitting the water. The maneuver probably saved her life by reducing the severity of the impact. The instructor passed over her a half second later. As he did, he flared to an almost complete stop and released his harness, dropping free of his glider and into the water next to the woman. While his glider fluttered off and fell into the water, the instructor swam to her, released her harness, and inflated her life jacket. Slipping his arm around her, he began to tow her towards shore. Halfway to shore, a rescue boat that had been dispatched from the shop found them and pulled them out of the water.

"How's that for drama?" Wally asked.

"Actually, that's not too bad," Kelly admitted. "A little too much detail for a summary, but, what the hell. You're new at this."

"Fuck you," Wally said.

"Yeah!" Kelly replied. "Make the woman who crashed be a college student – a hot one, of course – and after she gets rescued she thanks the instructor in ways that only a woman can!" Kelly laughed. "Sex sells, Wally! Sex sells!"

The Writer

"You're an ass," Wally said. "Just for that, I'm making the woman a nun who is in the islands on sabbatical."

Over Kelly's objections, Wally saved the summary and turned off the tablet.

"Alright," Wally announced. "Let's go see if you can do this."

Wally went downstairs and found the concierge at his podium near the front door of the hotel.

"Good morning!" the man said in a distinctly Bahamian accent.

"Good morning, Benjamin," Wally said, reading his name from the tag on his jacket. "I'd like to go hang gliding. There was a shop in the brochure that I picked up from the rack last night. Can you get me reservations and a cab?"

"Absolutely!" Benjamin smiled the smile of a man who just earned a commission. "Should I make lunch reservations at the Sandy Point restaurant as well? The food there is quite delicious and tastes especially fine after a morning of teasing the fates!"

"That would be nice. Thank you." Wally nodded. "I'll just wait for the cab over there."

"No need!" Benjamin announced. "There is a cab outside just waiting for a fare!"

Wally smiled and tipped Benjamin. "Thank you. If I don't come back, please check with the hospital."

"Oh! Ha! Ha!" Benjamin laughed, pocketed the tip and held the door to the cab for Wally. "You have a good time!"

The ride from Charlotte Amalie was the kind of ride that finds its way into commercials for travelers. The road wound its way around the sides of hills that fell steeply into the warm blue waters

The Writer

of the Caribbean Sea. Below, there were a few scattered villas, but most of the time the view was of far-away waves crashing silently on the rocky shore. Sailboats dotted the sea south of the main island. Little white clouds scudded across the deep blue sky making it all look more like a painting than a real view. Gazing out over this vista, Wally wondered to himself *what the hell is scudding, anyway?*

Kelly didn't know either, but advised Wally to look it up. If they were going to write novels, they would need to improve their vocabulary.

Off in the distance, Wally could see Buck Island and a few smaller ones as well. Way off in the distance, Wally thought he could see St. Croix, but he couldn't be certain. St. John, on the other hand, was very evident. The third of the US Virgin Islands came into view as the road made its final turn around the side of a hill and headed north along the east coast into Red Hook. St. John was just three miles away on the other side of Pillsbury Sound.

The view of Red Hook as the cab came around that last curve was stunning. The town itself was down at sea level and the road ahead dropped steeply into it. Wally could see the cliff on the other side of the marina. There were people already gliding through the air and more getting ready at the top. The cab wound its way through town and was getting pretty close to the shop when the cabbie slowed.

"What's going on?" Walter asked.

"There is a bit of a commotion on the beach," the cabbie replied. "See? All those people? They are just by the shop. I hope no one has been hurt."

The cabbie pulled up as close as he could and then asked Walter if he minded walking the last fifty yards. Wally said that the

130

The Writer

walk would be fine. After asking the cabbie to be sure to pick him up later that afternoon, he paid the fare and hiked to the shop.

The little hang gliding shop was exactly as he had described it in his summary. It was just a small building located right next to the beach. Wally had known that part from the brochure. He hadn't told Kelly though and Kelly thought that he'd made it up. Wally knew, though, that if writing well arose from writing about what you know about, then creativity wasn't really as much about inventing thigs as it was an ability to take vignettes from multiple experiences and stitch them together into a brand new story. His exercises of inventing stories for people who passed his toll booth had taught him that. The shop on the beach was something he knew about, so he included it.

Patting himself on the back while walking closer to the shop, he was struck with more than the fact that there seemed to be a lot of people there. There were certainly more than he expected. The underestimate soon became insignificant - It was the looks of concern and fear on the faces of the people that caught his attention. He was about to ask what was going on, when someone pointed out into the sound and hollered, "They've got her!"

Walter followed the pointed finger and saw a small skiff about a quarter mile offshore. There was debris in the water around it. As he watched, the man at the stern put the engine into gear and motored towards the shore. He ran the skiff aground on the sandy beach right by the shop and was greeted the exuberant cheers of the crowd.

"What's going on?" Walter asked a man standing next to him.

The Writer

"That woman," he said pointing to the people getting out of the boat, "she just fell from the sky. That man flew down after her and saved her. Then the boat went out to collect them both."

"My," Walter mused aloud. "What a coincidence."

"What?" the man asked.

"Oh. Nothing," Wally replied.

Slowly, the crowd dispersed and the beach returned to its normal state of being a tropical is and paradise. Another boat had gone out to retrieve whatever could be found of the gliders' wings. Other gliders were back in the air as if nothing had happened. Walter watched all of this with interest and, when things were back to normal, he walked to the shop

"What are you doing?" Kelly asked.

"You're going hang gliding," Wally replied.

"Did you see that?" Kelly objected. "This is dangerous. This is more drama than I want."

"Too bad," Wally said. "You need to conquer your fear."

Kelly realized that he was nct getting out of this and that the only way to go ahead with it was to rely on the self-confidence that Wally had given him.

"Okay." He gave in. "But if I die, I'm takin' you with me."

"Fair enough," Wally agreed.

Kelly got himself strapped in and lifted his feet as the instructor leapt off of the cliff and into the rising thermal. He swore that he'd never tell Wally, but he did close his eyes. Once in the air, though, he experienced the thrill and the peace of gliding. It was nothing

The Writer

like flying in that small airplane had been and it was nothing like the parachute jump. This was pure freedom. In no time at all, he was enjoying himself so much that he said, "Wally. Dude. You gotta buy me one of these."

"I'll buy one with the money from your first royalty check," Wally replied.

Kelly tried to capture every feeling, every emotion, and every nuance of fear that remained so that he could write about it later. He found it curious that even though the experience was completely different than flying in an airplane, there were still similarities.

"Hey Wally." Kelly roused his alter ego. "Guess what?"

"What?" Wally responded.

"You know how no matter how often you fly you still get a bit of the creeps when the plane hits an air pocket and bumps unexpectedly?" Kelly asked.

"Yeah. What of it?" Wally replied.

"There aren't any bumps, but I get the same feeling when the wind shifts and the wing drops or rises suddenly. I guess it's the unexpected nature of it, not the danger. Right?" Kelly continued to bother Wally.

"I guess," Wally said with exasperation. "I'm going to take a nap now. Please don't bother me."

"Okay," Kelly said grinning from ear to ear and enjoying the ride immensely.

Finally, the instructor dumped air from the wing and brought Kelly down. They landed on the sandy beach by the shop. Kelly made a mental note that the landing was very much like the landing

The Writer

he had experienced using the parachute. He thanked his instructor and wandered over to the Sand Point restaurant.

"Walter Fleegle," Wally announced as he approached the hostess stand. "I should have a reservation."

"Yes, Mr. Fleegle." The hostess couldn't have been more than sixteen or seventeen but she seemed to know what she was doing. Kelly made a mental note. Hostesses can be underage as long as they're cute. Waitresses are older because that job needs maturity. Bartenders must be 21. He'd need details like that if he ever wrote more than a summary.

"Benjamin called and said that you would be here after your flight. Most of the visitors like to talk about their experience afterwards so the shop has a permanent table here." Wally must have looked a little confused because the hostess continued to explain. "We put you at the glider's club table. You'll be sharing it with the other fliers, if that's alright."

Wally nodded and the young girl led him to a long table capable of serving ten. Only two were there, though; a man and a woman. "This'll be fine," Wally told the girl and took a seat.

Almost before he was fully seated, another young girl came over and asked if he would like a drink.

"Yes, please. Can I get a beer? Something on the light side?"

"See?" Kelly told Wally. "The waitress was at least twenty. Maybe older."

"Keep your own notes, Kelly," Wally said. He didn't want to get drawn into a conversation with Kelly at the moment. Instead he introduced himself to the other two people at the table.

The Writer

"Hi." The young man held out his hand to Wally. "I'm Bill Thorendahl. This is Pastor Melodie."

Melodie put her hand out to Wally. Noticing a few cuts and scrapes on her knuckles, he took it gently. "It's nice to meet you, Pastor."

"Oh, call me Melodie," she replied.

"You've got some nasty looking cuts on your hand. Have you had a rough day?" Wally asked. He was surprised when both Bill and Melodie began to laugh.

"You might say so!" Bill explained. "Melodie is the woman who fell from the sky today!"

"I'm lucky to be alive," she added, then corrected herself. "No. I'm blessed to be alive. Bill here saved me from drowning."

"Didn't you have a life jacket?" Wally asked.

"Sure, but I was unconscious and couldn't inflate it," Melodie explained.

"And you're a pastor?" Wally asked.

"Yes." Melodie smiled. "Lutheran. I was on my way back from the mission in Guyana and decided to stop and have some fun. I got more than I bargained for!"

The waitress brought Wally's beer and took his lunch order. He was lost in thought and almost didn't hear Melodie and Bill excuse themselves. "It was nice to meet you," she said.

"I have to get back to work," Bill said.

"And I have a plane to catch," Melodie added.

The Writer

Alone in the restaurant sipping his beer and nibbling on his fish sandwich, Wally struggled with the cosmic arguments for and against coincidence. Of course, Kelly had to butt in.

"Walter, Walter, Walter," Kelly began. "This morning you got up and wrote a summary as part of our experiment. Not an hour later, we get to Red Hook and find out that everything you wrote happened."

"Not true," Wally said. "Melodie wasn't a nun. Furthermore, Melodie didn't take Bill home and thank him the way you suggested."

"I hate to be a prick," Kelly started.

"But you still are," Wally interrupted.

"I hate to have to point this out, but you didn't actually write about Melodie thanking Bill or about her being a nun. You just talked about it." Kelly concluded his point.

Wally finished his lunch, paid the bill, and went to catch the cab back to the hotel. His argument with Kelly had subsided while he attended to these things. As soon as he was settled into the back seat, Kelly was back.

"A Lutheran pastor is close to a nun."

"They are not at all alike!" Wally rejected Kelly's suggestion. "A nun is ... forget it. I'm not going to discuss this."

"A nun is a religious woman. A pastor is a religious person ... who in this case is a woman," Kelly persisted.

"What if, to use your term, she had been a thankful woman?" Wally was drawn back into the argument.

The Writer

"Well, since you didn't write it down, the woman ended up being a religious person that is still allowed to have sex." Kelly pointed out the mixture of the two characters.

"She wouldn't have *thank you* sex." Wally fought back.

"No,." Kelly conceded the point. "And apparently she didn't. But she was thankful."

"Anybody would be!" Wally shot back.

"All I'm saying is that it's an awfully big coincidence," Kelly smirked.

"They happen all the time." Wally was determined to stop thinking about it and focused his eyes out of the cab window and onto the beautiful sparkling bay.

"Did you have a good day, sir?" Benjamin asked when Wally entered the lobby.

"It was interesting. Enjoyable and filled with drama," Wally replied.

"Yes," Benjamin remarked. "I heard about the commotion."

"Commotion!" Kelly exclaimed. "A woman is almost killed and he calls it a commotion?"

"Tourist town," Wally explained to Kelly. "Nothing bad happens. There are just little bits of commotion to make life interesting."

"I see," Kelly acknowledged as they entered the elevator.

Both Kelly and Wally were quiet momentarily as the elevator doors closed and they began to rise. Kelly broke the silence.

The Writer

"This is nothing like flying. You can feel that you're not on the ground, but it's nothing like flying."

"It isn't supposed to be," Wally muttered as he exited the elevator and walked to his room.

"Let's go see the tablet," Kelly suggested. "Maybe we'll find other points of coincidence."

"Maybe we'll find radical differences." Wally sat down on the bed and pushed the power button. "Look, Kelly. We were going hang gliding for the first time. You wanted drama. What could go wrong? Exactly what did go wrong? Losing air and having an equipment failure are probably the two most common causes of hang glider accidents. It's only logical. So it happened. If anything bad was going to happen, that was probably it. The coincidence is no more than the fact that an accident happened. That's not rare."

"I'm getting tired of arguing." Kelly admitted. "Would it also be coincidence that an instructor would crash his own glider to save her?"

"Totally!" Wally exclaimed. "Instructors are trained to save people! It's what they do! I bet that guy ..."

"Bill," Kelly interjected.

"... Bill," Wally repeated. "I bet that guy, Bill, even practiced that ditching maneuver before."

"You're probably right," Kelly conceded. "I hadn't thought about that."

The Writer

CHAPTER THIRTEEN

DREAMS

Thankful that Kelly had finally quit arguing, Walter made a few notes of his own on the tablet, brushed his teeth, and went to bed. Sleep was not kind to Walter that night. His dreams were a mixture of hang gliding, pistol shooting, race cars, and cheerleaders. The hang glider kept shifting back and forth between being a glider and a parachute. Sometimes he was with the instructor. Other times he was alone. Once he dreamed that he was the instructor and his student was a long-legged blonde cheerleader.

His race car dream suddenly turned into a police chase. Kelly was driving and Wally was hanging out the side window shooting at a bad guy. Then Kelly turned into the cheerleader and Wally was the driving instructor. At the end of the straightaway, the race car lifted off the ground and they flew away to an island in the Caribbean. Flying near the island, getting ready to land, they saw a boat that had crashed onto some rocks. There were women and children screaming for help. Wally had the cheerleader fly low and slow.

"I'm going to jump out and save them," he announced.

While he was putting on his parachute, the cheerleader – who was suddenly naked – told him. "If you survive, I'll have sex with you."

The Writer

"No thanks," Wally said, "I need love, not sex," and he jumped out of the airplane-car. As he floated down to execute his rescue, the airplane-race-car, turned into a flying-boat-race-car. The naked cheerleader circled the island and landed in the water nearby. Wally swam to shore, where he produced an inflatable life-raft from his hip pocket. He then saved the women and children, one of whom was a bridge player who thanked him for rescuing them. She then offered to gratify whatever carnal desire he had as her special thanks. Wally graciously declined and helped the women and children into the contraption piloted by the naked cheerleader. It had somehow become big enough to carry all the survivors, making it a flying-boat-race-bus. The naked cheerleader struggled to get the flying bus back into the air. Punching some numbers into a computer, she told Wally that they were 150 pounds too heavy to get airborne. Wally weighed 160 pounds and knew what he had to do. He jumped out of the plane to lighten the load. As he leapt, he could hear the naked cheerleader yelling, "That only makes me want you more!"

The flying-boat-bus lifted off into the air. The women and children had been saved. Wally treaded water and looked around to see if the life raft was still nearby. He spotted it about 200 yards away and began to swim. Somehow, he had cut himself during the rescue attempt. He wasn't bleeding very much but it was enough to attract a large shark that began to circle him. Pulling a SCUBA tank out of his other hip pocket, he put it on and swam to the bottom, where he speared a fish. Taking the fish off of the spear, he offered it to the shark. Of course the shark began to eat the fish and that gave Wally his chance to escape. Overhead, he could see the bottom of the life raft and he swam up to it. Tossing his SCUBA tank, mask, and fins into it, he looked down to see if the shark was

The Writer

coming up after him. He had nothing to worry about; it was still eating the fish. Wally heaved himself up into the life raft to find the naked cheerleader sitting on the other side.

"I'm glad you survived, Wally," she said with an impish grin. "Now get ready to have some fun."

Walter Fleegle woke up covered with sweat. He was breathing hard and his pulse was racing. Looking at the clock, he saw that it was 2:34 AM. He had to get more sleep. Kelly would be pissed if Wally didn't have the energy to go horseback riding on St. John in the morning. Wally showered in an attempt to cool down and remove the sweat, but that only served to make him even more awake. His dream still had him on edge. He'd never dreamed much at all before this and even when he had, he had never dreamed in such detail. He'd felt the vibrations of the race car and how they were lost when it lifted off the ground. He'd felt the impact of the water when he jumped from the airplane-bus. He had imagined every detail of the naked cheerleader's body, right down to those downy little hairs that grew on the side of her face, just in front of her temple. He had pictured her other temple in detail as well, but had pushed that image away.

Walter Fleegle needed a distraction in order to get back to sleep. Picking up the tablet, he decided to write the dream down. Maybe Kelly could use parts of it later when he began to write in earnest.

When he finished typing the story about his dream, Wally found that he was still thinking about the cheerleader. His dream had done more than give him an adrenaline rush, though. It had surfaced a deep desire that Wally had suppressed for too many years. Walter really didn't want to get laid for the sake of getting

The Writer

laid. He'd already explained that to Kelly several times and in his dream he had said the same thing to the naked cheerleader. Wally wanted a woman. He wanted a companion and a partner. He would have sex with her: a real woman, not a fantasy.

Walter Fleegle began to write it all down.

Walter Finds a Woman - by Walter Fleegle

Summary: [Note to self- get to the summary later, write about how Wally meets Tatum.]

Walter Fleegle ambled somewhat aimlessly through the grocery store. He had just completed his shift at the tollbooth and still wore his Florida-shirt uniform provided by the DOT. Walter was oblivious, as he had been for more than twenty years, to the other people in the store.

Walter deleted the last sentence, and continued.

Walter was keenly aware of people. He saw them every day at the toll booth. He saw lots of different people and imagined lots of different stories, one for each of them. In the store with him there was a mother with a newborn child. She was smiling. There was also a mother with five children, all between the ages of five and eleven. She was not smiling. She was herding. The oldest child tried to help. Walter

The Writer

stopped his own search for groceries and reached a box of cereal down from the top shelf for a woman in her sixties. In the next aisle, he helped a man with a walker read the price on a package of boneless, skinless chicken. All of those people were typical of the people that Wally usually observed at the market. The most interesting story that Wally attached to these people was the one for the old man. He wore a Navy ball cap that had "Iwo Jima" stitched onto it. Other shoppers were of the more common types: college kids, a man in a suit, a construction crew picking up fruit juice and water.

Only one other shopper had caught Walter's eye. She was elegant and sexy at the same time. Taller than Wally by several inches, she was the kind of woman who made people stare. Most of the stares were furtive: stolen glances at their briefest and lustful glares when she wouldn't notice. Her hair was on the short side for a woman, but it was the most lustrous red that Wally had ever seen. She wore a tight white spandex shirt; the kind that women wear to the gym. Her shorts were just as flattering. They were also spandex but they were black. She had the kind of body that only a very regular workout routine coupled with good genetics could create. There were a thousand stories that Walter could make up about her, but the one that kept coming to mind was one that would explain why it seemed that she was following him. She had been in the coffee aisle. She was there

The Writer

when he got the cereal for the old woman. She saw him help the veteran. He knew that because he had caught her smiling.

Walter corrected himself. This goddess of the gymnasium wasn't exactly following him, but she was often in the same aisle as he was. Wally fought back his distraction when he got to the cold case where they kept the cheese. Walter needed to find a special cheese for a special recipe. It called for cheese made from sheep milk. He'd had goat cheese on many occasions but had heard that cheese from sheep was slightly different.

Walter was completely lost in thought as he examined the cheeses in the specialty case. Should he get the Halloumi? Walter looked closely at the label. The cheese was imported from Cyprus which made sense. That was where that type of cheese originated. But the ingredients listed a mixture of goat and sheep milk. He put it back. Next to it were three others cheeses with a picture of sheep on the label. Two were Italian (Pecorino Romano and Pecorino Tuscano). The last was a French Roquefort. He decided on the Tuscano.

Wally reached his hand into the case. Just as he picked up the packet of Tuscano, the slender fingers of a woman's hand touched the back of his own. For a second, they stayed there, touching him softly. The moment ended with her voice almost whispering in his

The Writer

ear. "I'm so sorry!" she exclaimed rather quietly. "I guess we were going for the same thing!"

Walter Fleegle looked to his right to see who it was who had chosen the same unusual cheese. It was the grocery goddess. She was even more stunning standing next to him than she had been when he saw her at the other end of the aisle. Walter was instantly captivated, immobilized as if he had been a tiny fish captured by a sea anemone. Her deep green eyes were her tentacles and Wally was unable to break free. To Wally, her eyes glimmered and danced as if they had fairies living in them; fairies throwing a party. Smiling, he managed to stammer a few words.

"Oh. Excuse me." Wally handed her the cheese. "You take it. I'll get another."

"This is the last one," she said softly. "You take it."

Wally didn't even bother to look at the case. It didn't matter. "That's okay. I'll take the Pecorino."

"I can't let that happen." The woman smiled sweetly. "I'll tell you what. I'll take it on one condition."

Wally's eyebrows went up as if to inquire what the condition might be.

"You come to my place and tell me how well I did in preparing the dinner. It's a new recipe and I'm a

The Writer

little nervous. I can try it out on you before I serve it to anyone else."

"We've only just met." Walter started to try to back out. His uncertainty and self-esteem problems were raging within him. He'd been working on getting better for several months and had thought he was on the way to recovery – until now. Staring at the lovely woman with green eyes, clad in her professional-grade black and white spandex outfit, he was emotionally crashing into the depths of self-doubt. "Aren't you afraid that I might be a ...?" Walter was trying to find the right word. He didn't want to say *bad man* but *rapist* and *murderer* didn't really sound much better.

"Are you asking me if I should be talking to strangers?" She laughed. Walter thought it was the most melodious pleasant laugh he had ever heard. "I'm a pretty good judge of character," she added. "I think I can feel safe with you."

What Walter heard wasn't the comfort that she had intended, but that she was fit and worked out, while she saw Wally as being frail and weak. What he heard was consistent with how he saw himself and not necessarily how she had seen him. What he heard was that if he was a bad man, she felt that she could kick his ass. He swallowed hard and nodded. "Okay. Deal."

146

The Writer

"Good!" she exclaimed. "My name's Tatum. What's yours?"

"I'm Walter," he replied. "Walter Fleegle."

The two shoppers exchanged phone numbers and addresses, then said goodbye and went their separate ways. He would be at her place for dinner the day after tomorrow.

Walter Fleegle read through his story about how he would meet his true love and smiled. Shutting off the tablet, he snuck back into bed. For the rest of the night, he dreamed about dancing green eyes and spandex workout clothing. The blonde cheerleader had gone away.

CHAPTER FOURTEEN

A PRIMER IN CREATIVE WRITING

In the morning, Wally woke up strangely refreshed. His dreams – both the weird one and the nice one – were still in his memory, but neither one bothered him. He had written notes about his first weird dream. Writing about meeting Tatum had precipitated his second dream.

"Can you use any of that?" he asked Kelly.

"Probably." Kelly was lost in his own thoughts. "When do you think I should start writing something in earnest? We've done a lot of things. If your weird dream last night is any indication, we probably have enough experiences to put something together." Kelly paused. "Hey, Wally. Why did you write about what a wimp you are? You wrote about it, so I know that you know how you see yourself. You invented me, so I know you want to change that. Why write about it?"

"I just thought that by writing it down, I could start to overcome it," Walter explained. "The truth is that you've already been more daring and dashing than I've ever been. I think it's working."

Kelly nodded. "I guess it's along the same lines as a twelve step program. Acceptance has to come first."

The Writer

With that settled, Walter got around to answering Kelly's question. "I think you could start writing something anytime you want. We don't have to go horseback riding. We could go sit on the beach under an umbrella; drink tea until noon and Daiquiris until dinner while you compose on the tablet."

"I kinda like that idea," Kelly said. "Let's see what I've got. We can go to St. John tomorrow."

Kelly started to think about what to write. He got nowhere.

"You're trying too hard," Wally advised.

"How do you try too little?" Kelly remarked. "Actually, you would know a lot about that, wouldn't you?"

"That was mean!" Wally shouted. "I'm working on it!"

"Sorry. I just meant that I don't know how to do this." Kelly shook his head. "I wrote a couple summaries, but nothing substantial. You're the one with the education."

"Right," Wally mused. "Try this. First invent a character; like I did with you. Then put the character in a time and a place. If you do a good job with the character, then he will just react to whatever is going on and you don't have to think as much."

"Don't I need a plot?" Kelly inquired.

"Have you read some of the shit that's out there?" Wally laughed. "But, sure, you can have a sketchy sort of a plot if you want."

"What do I need?" Kelly was still uncertain.

"You need a good guy, a bad guy, a love interest, and a quest." Wally listed the elements he had learned in his creative writing class twenty years earlier.

The Writer

Kelly looked at him sort of funny. "That's it?"

"Pretty much." Walter continued to explain. "The good guy can be one person or a platoon. The platoon can be army guys, lawyers, protestors, or Boy Scouts. Men or women, adults or kids, even dogs or cats can be the good guys. Same with the bad guys. The love interest can be between a man and a woman, a kid and a horse, an explorer and the horizon, an addict and his drug. It doesn't matter. It's the quest that makes the story."

"You're full of shit." Kelly snorted.

"Nope. Not at all," Wally said. "Take the ancient Greek tome: *Jason and The Argonauts: the Golden Fleece.* Jason and his boys are the good guys. There are many bad guys, but the two main ones are the two kings. The love interest is Hera, the queen of the gods. She had a thing for Jason. The quest is that one king sends Jason to steal the Golden Fleece from the other one. The rest of the story is made up of the adventures that the good guys have to go on in order to complete the quest. Each adventure has its own set of bad guys and that keeps the story moving."

Kelly was not convinced.

"Okay," Wally continued. "Take any 007 book. Bond is the good guy. Bad guys are abundant. That guy with the gold fangs was every bit as bad as the Cyclops in *The Odyssey*. Miss Moneypenny provides the love interest, but Bond is too busy screwing everything else that moves to notice. That allows for sequels. Usually after the love interest is settled, the book ends. You know? Happily ever after and all that shit? The quest is usually to kill the bad guys or steal something – which is what spies do."

"Unbelievable." Kelly shook his head. "What about non-fiction?"

The Writer

"Oh, for Christ's sake. Sign up for a class." Wally was exasperated. "Just get going."

"So the only thing I need to do that's really creative is to create this person, this character?" Kelly wanted to make sure he understood.

"Right." Wally nodded. "And when you do, you don't need to tell the reader everything. Your character just needs to be very well defined in your mind."

"Like Tatum?" Kelly laughed. "She had pretty good definition."

Wally threatened to turn off the tablet.

Kelly got to work.

"Man or woman?" He made a list of questions.

"Age?"

"Build, height, hair color, eye color?"

Wally complimented him. "That's right. You need all that even if you never tell it to the reader. The character has to be as real to you as I am."

Kelly went on with his list.

"Skills? Employment? Level of education? Military, civilian, bureaucrat? Employer, employee, retired?"

Wally interrupted. "Don't forget his character traits."

Kelly nodded. "Is he honest? He's the good guy, so yes. Is he self-confident? Is he outgoing or an introvert? Does he have bad habits at all? Is he a smoker? Does he drink? Is he a sex addict?"

"He's the good guy," Wally reminded him.

The Writer

"Bond was the good guy," Kelly countered.

"Bond screwed all those women in the service of his country," Wally explained.

"But sex sells!" Kelly objected.

Wally shook his head. "Being a sex addict is a little over the top. Unless you want to write a romance novel."

Kelly continued his list. "Is he the kind of guy who goes to church?"

"Stop asking questions and start building the character," Wally advised.

Kelly typed furiously as he made his choices. When he finished, he asked himself what it was that Wally said was next.

"Situation." Wally supplied the missing word.

Kelly nodded and began to think of sticky situations. Maybe his Mercedes broke down in south Chicago on a Saturday night. Maybe his car broke down in Morocco. Maybe it was a Land Rover in the Savannah of South Africa and he was surrounded by lions.

"Do I have to tell the situation?" he asked. "I mean right at the beginning?"

"No," Wally said after reflecting for a moment. "You can introduce the situation slowly."

"Okay. Let me play with this," he replied.

"Did you want to go to the beach?" Wally asked.

"No. Too many bikinis down there. I don't want any distractions." Kelly started typing.

The Writer

"One more thing," Wally interrupted. "The first few sentences need to be grabbers. A lot of people will open a book to the first page and read a little bit. If they like the first paragraph, you've made a sale."

Kelly went back to typing. For ten minutes, he typed and erased, typed and erased. Finally, he seemed somewhat happy.

<u>Working Title: Ice</u>

Eddie opened his eyes to find himself staring at a wall of ice. He was cold, but not as cold as he thought he should be. *How cold should I be?* he asked himself as he tried to drag himself back to consciousness. He needed to remember where he was and how he got there. He was completely encased in ice, but there was room enough to move. He could even turn around with a little effort. The ice off to his left was a deep purple while the ice to his right was a lighter blue.

As his brain tried desperately to recapture reality, Eddie took inventory. He was wearing a full cold-weather survival suit. It was white with gray splotches on it. He thought that was an odd color choice, but was soon distracted by the other equipment he apparently owned: an ice pick, crampons, some rope, and a rifle. *Come on, Eddie!* he screamed to himself, "*Time to wake up and remember!*

The Writer

Kelly looked at Wally. "What d'ya think?"

"I see you went right to the situation." Wally nodded. "Not bad, though. Not bad at all. You've got a character. I suppose the first quest is to get out of the ice. Have you got anything in mind for bad guys? A love interest?"

Kelly was perturbed. "Not yet. I need to do one thing at a time!"

"Any idea where this is going?" Wally asked.

"Well, first he has to get out of the ice. Otherwise the story's over." Kelly laughed at his own joke. "The deep purple ice is going to be thin and he's going to use his pick to break out. It's purple because there's water on the other side, so I guess he'll almost drown, then almost freeze. His love interest can save him from freezing, I guess. Or he can save himself and I'll introduce the love interest later on. Besides, I think the bad guys need to be introduced sooner. They're the ones that somehow got him stuck in the ice in the first place. Once we have the bad guys, I suspect that we'll come up with the quest."

"Did you notice how you started saying we instead of I?" Wally asked with a grin.

"No. But now that you mention it, I guess I did." Kelly grimaced. "Maybe Eddie will have amnesia for a while. His love interest can help bring him out of it and that's when we reveal the quest. How's that?"

"You just made an outline." Wally smiled. "I'm going to make a writer out of you … I mean us … yet."

The Writer

"Should I do that now?" Kelly asked.

"What?" Wally replied.

"Should I prepare an outline?" Kelly wondered why he always had to be so specific.

"You can make a sequence of milestones or important events so that the story makes sense, but it has to be flexible. Remember, the story is going to rely on how Eddie reacts to different things that happen. If you over-manage that, then the story can become stilted or contrived," Wally explained.

Wally and Kelly never did get over to St. John to go horseback riding. Kelly spent every waking moment typing, erasing, and typing some more. Before Wally knew it, the day had come when he had to go back to work. He didn't mind. Kelly was enjoying himself, and Wally actually missed working in the toll booth. He missed making up little vignettes about the people who drove through and he missed looking down the shirts of the young girls. His vacation had taught him a lot about himself. Kelly had taught Wally a lot about Wally. Walter Fleegle was creative. Kelly's obsession about wanting to fuck the cheerleaders was actually a suppressed desire on Wally's part to have a relationship. The voyeurism he practiced in his tollbooth had been a cheap surrogate. After reading what he had written about Tatum, Walter knew that it was time for him to find a woman. His refusals of the cheap sex that had been offered – even if they had been make-believe – taught him that he wanted a partner, not just a good time.

155

CHAPTER FIFTEEN

A ROUGH DRAFT

For the next three weeks, Kelly was up to all hours of the morning working on his first novel. He had decided to stay with his opener.

Ice - by Kelly Blanton

Summary: Eddie had pick-axed his way through the thin ice only to find himself drowning as the near freezing water rushed into his cocoon. Struggling free, he swam to the surface popping up at the edge of an ice floe. He had to get out of the water, so he used his pick for leverage. Slamming it into the edge of the ice, he hauled himself up onto a sheet of ice that was about 200 yards long and fifty yards wide. He thought he would certainly freeze until he remembered his survival training. He quickly emptied what little water there was that had leaked into his survival suit, wrung out his clothing and got back into the suit. Then he peed in his suit. The pee didn't really warm him up, but it brought some of the inner heat to the surface and it made him feel warmer.

The Writer

Eddie was picked up by a helicopter from one of those tours that take people from Kansas out into the Bering Sea to look at glaciers. He had no identification and no idea who he was or how he got there. After he was released from the hospital, where he met Barbara, he went on his quest to find out who he was and how he ended up in the ice coffin. Barbara was a nurse at the hospital. She took an interest in both Eddie and his predicament, letting him stay at her apartment and paying his expenses as he sought his identity. Starting with the newspapers, he scoured every source of information that he could find looking for reports of missing persons, downed aircraft, or sunken ships. The most important clues that he had were the things that he had with him. An internet search led him to believe that his grey and white clothing had been some sort of camouflage. The pattern didn't match anything that the military had. It didn't match anything in the outdoor catalogs either. It had to be rare, custom, or perhaps foreign. His other equipment was pretty high-tech stuff but there was nothing that indicated where he got it or even who had manufactured it – except for the rifle. It was a Remington model 700, but it had been highly modified.

Eddie and Barbara concluded that he must have gotten it from a very low-profile source; a source that had the equipment custom made for their own use.

The Writer

They had been just about ready to give up, when Barbara and Eddie saw an investigative special on the nature channel. It was about people who hunted polar bears. One group, an illegal one, was offering secret hunting trips to rich people who wanted their own rug. The trips were arranged on the internet and even the highly paid investigators were unable to find the owners. The other side of the story, the part that made the special so very interesting, was that an eco-terrorist group had started hunting the hunters. A camouflage uniform just like the one that Eddie had worn had been found abandoned on an ice floe next to the skinless body of a bear. The question was who had left it there.

Barbara and Eddie had started to fall in love just before this news was discovered, and now they were both afraid. Barbara had fallen in love with Eddie first and had invited him to her bed. Their lovemaking had been passionate, tender, and intense. The shadow of fear that had now befallen them was born of wondering if Eddie was part of the group that hunted bears or a part of the one that hunted the hunters. Barbara wasn't sure if she could sleep with Eddie any more no matter which one he was.

Eddie tracked down the people who had made the documentary and hounded them until he had as many answers as he thought he could get. The most relevant answer that he got was that the 90 minute show was

The Writer

based on about three minutes of fact and 87 minutes of speculation. Eddie took his three minutes home to Barbara's apartment and started to conduct his own investigation. Before long, Barbara noticed that Eddie had skills: investigative skills. He couldn't remember who he was, but she was convinced that whatever he did, it involved finding answers.

Both Barbara and Eddie were relieved when Eddie concluded his quest. After following lead after lead, Eddie learned that he was a private investigator from northern California. He had been hired by the very wealthy parent of a missing 23 year old college student who was also an environmental activist. His client had supplied the clothing, the survival suit, the axe, and the rifle. The client's daughter had gone to the Aleutians to try to document the polar bear hunts. Eddie had been worried that she was part of the group that hunted the bears, but his client assured him that this was not possible. Eddie and Barbara now knew who he was and why he was in Alaska, but they still didn't know how he got stuck in the ice or where the girl was.

"How are you going to end it?" Wally asked Kelly.

"I'm not sure." Kelly was actually stumped. Wally's advice of building a character and putting him in a situation had worked pretty well as far as it went. It didn't help him figure out how Eddie had gotten into the situation in the first place.

The Writer

"I say we start sending letters to agents and publishers," Wally said.

"You know our chances are like a billion to one," Kelly replied sadly. "I want to finish this first."

Wally considered Kelly's point. "You know? You're right. I was doing a little research on how to get something published and things aren't like the way they used to be."

"What do you mean?" Kelly frowned.

"Once upon a time, a guy would write a book, send it in, and if the publisher liked it, he printed it and marketed it. Now, if we want to do this, we basically have to buy our success," Wally explained. "Look at my notes. I got them from about a hundred websites. Publishers have become completely risk-averse. If you want something published, you pay for it. No one works on commission or percentage anymore. The sad part is that even after the author pays the freight the publisher still gets a percentage. What a racket."

"What do we do?" Kelly was distraught. "No! Don't tell me! That shit's your problem. I'm the writer and you're the publicist and agent. You just get it done!"

"Great," Wally muttered. " created an artist with an attitude and a temper." Wally took Kelly by the throat. "I can rewrite you, ya know."

"Alright." Kelly settled down. "I'll behave."

"Look," Wally said more calmly. "Most of these people have a process where you have to qual fy just to hire them. They don't take just anybody's money."

The Writer

Kelly winced.

Wally continued. "Most of them don't want much more than the first couple chapters and a summary. You already wrote a really good summary, so why don't you work up chapter one and let's start sending stuff in. We'll use the shotgun approach."

Kelly nodded and momentarily went back to work. "How long is a chapter?"

"Good question." Wally started flipping through his notes. "It turns out that there are two basic options. One is that each chapter is five pages, more or less, and they should all be the same length. The other is to just write the story and put a chapter break in where it makes sense."

"I like that last one," Kelly said. "I've read some of the other kind and chapters always seem to be rushed or stretched out like a … what. Tell me something that stretches a lot."

"Hmm…" Wally scratched his head. "Like a tattoo on an old lady."

"Forget it." Kelly rejected the metaphor. "How… where, do I break the chapter?"

"I'd say that you go until Eddie pulls himself up onto the ice for the first time. The reader gets to go from Eddie being certain to die to Eddie having small a chance of survival." Wally pointed to the summary to show Kelly what he meant. "Then chapter two can be the rescue. Start with him wringing out his clothes and end when he gets to the hospital. He can meet Barbara in chapter three and you can start working the love interest into the story."

"I know a great joke about two nurses." Kelly smiled.

The Writer

"Filler," Wally said flatly.

"It's a really good joke though!" Kelly objected.

"Oh, jeez." Wally sighed. "Go ahead."

Kelly was giddy. "You see, there were these two nurses who worked in the recovery ward at the hospital. One of them was quite pretty and the other was sort of on the unattractive side."

"She was ugly?" Wally interrupted.

"I'm trying to be gentle. You know, politically correct? There are no ugly people." Kelly went on with his joke. "The patient – that can be Eddie – had been in the hospital for a few days recovering from his ordeal. One day the less than attractive nurse gave him his sponge bath. When she came back out to the nurse's station, she told the pretty nurse that the patient was awake and that he had a very interesting tattoo. It was on his penis. Apparently the patient had a girlfriend or wife name Mona and had her name tattooed there. The pretty nurse said that she needed to see this for herself, so the next day she made sure that she was the one to give Eddie a sponge bath. When she came out, she told the first nurse that the tattoo was indeed unusual. It didn't say *Mona* though. It said *Memento of a visit to Las Vegas Nevada*."

Wally looked at Kelly in total disbelief. "We are not putting that in the book."

Kelly went to work on chapter one.

For the next week, Kelly wrote and Wally made up characters from his toll booth.

The Writer

CHAPTER SIXTEEN

QUERY

"It's ready," Kelly announced.

"Good," Wally replied. "So am I. While you were writing, I was collecting lists of publishers and agents. We can get this thing emailed out in less than an hour to 87 different places."

"What if no one likes it?" Kelly asked timidly.

"That could happen. Maybe no one will," Wally said. "But if only one of them does, then we're on to the next step. If no one does, then we went skydiving, flying, shooting, sailing, SCUBA diving, parachuting, and hang gliding. That alone is more fun than I've had in twenty years."

"I see your point," Kelly muttered. "Anyway, the files are right there on the tablet. Do your thing."

"What should I do while you're doing that?" Kelly asked.

"You could write the rest of *Ice* or you could start the next book," Wally said as he prepared the files for transmission.

Kelly was still stuck on how to get Eddie into the ice, so he decided to start the next book. It was difficult, because Wally was using the tablet to send emails, but somehow they managed.

The Writer

<u>Working Title: The Intern - by Kelly Blanton</u>

Chapter One

Bodies were everywhere; literally everywhere. The bloated vestiges of what had once been alive bubbled as gas leaked from their intestines. The bubbles coalesced, creating a foam that covered the water of the small pond. Slimy and already stinking, the dead were piled up on top of each other. The skin was shiny from the goo that had oozed out and each body sparkled in the afternoon sun. The scene was surreal.

A local farmer had been the first to call in a report of the carnage. He had been afraid to touch the bodies. It was a good thing he hadn't. They were so bloated that they seemed as if they might explode with the slightest provocation. Clint Seston crouched at the bank and pulled one of the bodies to shore. He wished that he had been assigned something different, but this was his job and he would do it. His meticulously pressed uniform would certainly never be the same after today.

With his face scrunched up trying to keep the smell from making him puke, he looked over at his partner and said, "It looks like a small bass to me." Clint dropped the fish into a plastic baggie. "There are a couple blue-gill over there. Can you reach them?"

The Writer

Leslie used a stick to drag the rotting fish to shore and dropped them into the bag with the bass. Clint was a senior biologist with the Game and Fish Commission. Today he had the double honor of investigating a fish kill and babysitting the new intern, Leslie Cotton.

"All done," Wally announced.

"I'm still working," Kelly muttered.

"We should hear back from someone soon." Wally smiled.

Ding. The tablet announced that an email had been received.

"What's it say?" Kelly asked.

> *Dear Kelly Blanton. Thank you for your query. As you know we receive hundreds of query letters every day. Please allow two to four months for us to get back to you. We appreciate your patience.*

Wally started to cry as he read it to Kelly.

"Look at it this way," Kelly said cheerfully. "It'll give me time to write more stories before we have to go on tour!"

Kelly's attitude was antithetical to Wally's and it made Wally laugh.

The Writer

"I'm getting a beer. Successful or not, we reached a milestone today and I'm going to celebrate."

Wally thought about offering Kelly one, but dismissed the idea thinking, *Kelly needs to write some more.*

The Writer

CHAPTER SEVENTEEN

DEALING WITH REJECTION

Once again, Walter woke up in a sweat. It was 2AM. Three weeks had gone by since he sent the query letters. During the day, he had dutifully gone to his job and during the evening Kelly had dutifully been working on *The Intern.* The dream that had awakened Wally was about publishers. He kept dreaming about them reading Kelly's sample chapters and laughing. They laughed and laughed until someone finally typed the email sending the book back.

We're sorry, sir, we just don't see a good fit between your manuscript and our company profile.

Wally tried to pretend that it was Kelly who was being rejected, but he failed. It was him. He knew the trick he had been playing on himself and the failure was his. Kelly was innocent.

Wally needed to get back to sleep. The feeling of failure and sadness, however, was too much. He knew that he would need to conquer that before lying down again.

The Writer

Wally turned on the tablet, and found the story he had started about meeting Tatum. In the story, he had just agreed to have dinner with her. That's where he would start writing again.

Walter Fleegle was scared and excited. He was going on his first date in more than twenty years. The only way he could come to grips with his fear was to deny that it was a date at all. He kept telling himself that he had met a nice lady in the grocery store. They obviously both shared a love of cheese and of cooking. Walter convinced himself that she had been telling the truth when she had joked that he would be her guinea pig; she would try out her new recipe on someone insignificant before she served it to important guests.

He had succeeded, but still didn't want to look like a fool, so he put on one of his new suits, stopped for a small, noncommittal bouquet of flowers, picked up a nice Sonoma wine and drove his scooter to Tatum's apartment.

When she opened the door, he immediately knew that he had totally overplayed his hand. He was totally overdressed. Tatum beamed at him like a west coast light house. Her green eyes sparkled and wrapped him up like a warm breeze. She invited him in and took the flowers, adding, "These certainly are nice, and you look very nice too."

The Writer

Wally, in his suit and tie, still holding the bottle of expensive wine looked at Tatum, trying to capture her essence. She was as casually dressed as he was nicely dressed. Cut-off jeans, a man's button down dress shirt with the sleeves rolled up and fuzzy mouse slippers put her attire about as far to the other end of the fashion spectrum as she could get.

Somehow, though, it didn't seem to matter. He was only uncomfortable for that split second before she looked into his eyes.

Suddenly Wally was at a loss about what to write. He had set the stage for a romantically funny evening at Tatum's apartment. There was wine. She was sexy. He was handsome and comfortable. The evening could go anywhere.

So Wally turned off the tablet and went back to bed.

Every day for the next week, Wally would go to work, return home, check his email and read rejection letter after rejection letter.

Every night during that same time, Wally would wake up at 2AM worried about his future. Every night, he would write a little more about his date with Tatum. Even though she was completely fictional, she seemed to have a calming effect on him. She seemed to make things right.

On one night, he had told her that he was undergoing a career change from toll booth worker to novelist. He wrote that she had refrained from telling him how hard it was to break into the field.

The Writer

She didn't ridicule him or make him feel that he wouldn't be successful. She even liked the idea of writing under a pen name. The one thing she did that he was uncomfortable with was to ask to read some of his writing. He couldn't tell her that she was just his imagination, so he let her read the beginning of *Ice*.

"I sent this off to 87 publishers and so far I have 68 rejections," Wally told her while they had a glass of after-dinner wine.

"Don't worry," she comforted him. "It's really quite good and someone will realize that soon."

It made no difference to Wally that he was writing the words for Tatum to speak. He still found them soothing.

When Saturday morning broke, Walter Fleegle had spent the wee hours of six nights writing about the events of a single evening with Tatum. At the end of last night's entry, he had started to leave, when Tatum gently pulled him back and softly kissed his cheek.

"Everything's going to be alright," she said.

He sure hoped so. This Saturday morning he had made plans to give Kelly another experience to write about. Kelly was going to school to get his motorcycle endorsement on his driver's license. Wally thought it would be easy, since he had ridden his scooter to work for more than ten years. Unlike most of his other expectations, this time Wally was right. Kelly blew through the class and the test with ease and by four o'clock, Wally had his motorcycle license.

Kelly had to talk him into it, but on the way home from the training center, Wally stopped at the Triumph dealer and bought a brand new Bonneville. It was a mid-sized cruiser-style bike and that suited Wally just fine. Anything larger and his small frame would

The Writer

have had trouble holding it up. Anything smaller wouldn't have been much different than his scooter. Walter put fifty miles on the bike before he even thought about taking it home. This, he decided, would be the new Walter Fleegle. No more scooters. No more dull and boring.

Wally was flying down a four lane road and feeling really good when he saw the bookstore. In an instant, he decided that he needed to break out of the rut that he had constructed for himself with his late night writing. In that same instant, however, he had passed the store. Not to be deterred by his slow reaction time, he slowed, made a u-turn, and pulled into the parking lot. Wally was going to buy a book to read, instead of playing at writing one.

Locking his helmet onto his bike, he sat there for a minute, thinking. The last couple of hours had really been good for him. Not only did he like the freedom of being on a bike, but straddling the bike was such a different experience than sitting on a scooter. He thought it must be the body position. On a scooter, he had to sit the same way that he had when he was in time-out as a kid. Knees together, back straight, looking straight ahead. Sure, his hands were on the controls instead of his knees, but the position was essentially the same. On the bike he felt like a grown-up.

The feeling was enhanced as he walked past the big glass windows on the way into the bookstore. Noticing his reflection in the windows, he decided that he didn't cut such a bad figure. What had been previously seen as minor incongruities in how his face was structured were suddenly very much in line with the stereotypical biker face. His limp had been corrected by his special insert. The black leather jacket hadn't been adorned with any patches, but it was still pretty impressive. He smiled as he went in, wondering how many bikers frequent book stores.

The Writer

The store was one of the big box stores and must have contained a hundred thousand books. Wally went straight to the mystery section and began to browse. The store was almost empty, as most of them are for most of the day, and true to his training in the toll booth, Wally took note of everyone there.

"It's quiet today," he said to the young man who asked if he needed help.

"You might not expect it," the sales associate replied, "but bookstores have busy and quiet periods just like restaurants."

Wally had been looking at mysteries for a few minutes when he noticed a newcomer. The woman who entered the store was slender, blonde, and quite pretty without being over-the-top. He added her to his mental tally of customers and continued to browse. On a whim, he moved to the military history section. Wally thought that Kelly might want a book on guns or ammunition so that he would have the right details if he needed them for a story.

From there he wandered to the history section to see if there were books on criminals, the mob, or Congress that Kelly could use. It was odd, he thought, that the blonde girl always seemed to be one aisle away. She never made eye contact when he glanced at her, but on occasion, he thought he caught her glancing at him. He couldn't be sure, because all he really had was an impression created by his peripheral vision.

Earlier, when he noticed her come in, Wally had put her in the pretty category, but he could now see that she could be quite beautiful with the right hair and clothing. *Blondie*, as he had tagged her, was tall – perhaps 5'8" – and slender. Her hair was short and tightly curled, but it didn't have that stiff look that some tight curls have. It was loose and bouncy. He saw her smile as she read

The Writer

something on a book jacket. It was a nice smile. Wally catalogued all of this information for use later as a potential character. He realized that he was doing the same thing that he did every day in the toll booth. The difference was that today he was in a bookstore.

Wally put her out of his mind and drifted over to the specialty section of the store. Maybe he could find a more up-to-date writer's guide than the one he had at home. Lost in the intensity of his examination of the books lined up on the shelf, he failed to notice that Blondie had moved into the same aisle. He failed to notice her standing next to him looking at the same shelf. He failed to notice her reaching for the same book that he had selected. His hand and her hand arrived at the book at the same time.

"Oh, I'm so sorry!" Blondie said. "I didn't mean to do that!"

"That's okay," Wally replied. "I was so engrossed that I didn't even see you."

"Is that the book you want?" she asked. "Or are you just looking at it?"

Wally smiled a crooked smile. "I won't know if it's the one I want until I look at it, now will I?"

"No," she conceded. "I guess not."

"Is it the one you want?" he asked.

"Not if you want it." She pointed at the shelf. "It's the last copy." Blondie looked directly into Wally's eyes for the first time. "Are you a writer?"

"I'm a wanna-be." Wally handed her the book. "Are you?"

The Writer

"Actually, I'm an editor. Sort of." Blondie stammered a bit. "I do a little part-time work like that. It's not really a career, but what do you do with a degree in English Composition?"

Wally laughed. "Don't I know it! I have the same problem!"

Blondie smiled. "A wanna-be, huh?"

"Yeah," Wally explained. "I've got twenty years in at my current job and am looking at a pretty comfortable retirement, so I thought I'd try and write the great American novel. I know it's silly of me but…"

Blondie put her hand on his arm. "No! Don't ever think that. You need to be persistent. From what I've read …" Blondie held up the writer's guide. "… in books like this, the key to success is never giving up. Of course you have to have something good, but being good is not good enough. The key is to keep at it."

Wally nodded in acceptance of her theory.

Blondie's expression changed from concern to curiosity. "I saw you in the military section. Are you going to write about the service?"

Wally shook his head. "I was looking for a good reference book on firearms. I just bought a new gun and thought I might develop a little background knowledge in case I needed it for a book someday."

"That's a good idea! Do your research before you actually need it!" Blondie smiled. "I'll tell you what," Blondie said. "I'll buy the guide. I'll take it home and read it, making notes as I do. Then I'll give it to you."

"That sounds like a good deal, but let me pay half," Wally said.

The Writer

"Fair enough," Blondie agreed. "Now give me your name and phone number so I can call you when I'm done with it."

Wally did as she had suggested, adding a twenty dollar bill to the paper with his name, and watched her bounce up to the checkout counter. The last few minutes had perplexed him. He had had a subtle, but persistent, sense of déjà vu during the entire exchange.

Shaking the cobwebs of surrealism out of his head, he meandered back to the mystery section and picked out something by a new and unknown author. Seeing the name on the book and realizing that he didn't recognize it, Wally also realized that he didn't know Blondie's name either. He had just given a total stranger twenty dollars and had no idea if he would ever see her or his half of the book again. Wally decided to tell Kelly about how a con artist can get books for half price. Maybe he could use it.

CHAPTER EIGHTEEN

JACQUELINE

The next morning, Wally got up and checked his email: another rejection. Rejection on a Sunday morning was not to be taken as a good omen. On the other hand, he realized that ever since he had returned from St. Thomas, there had been no cats in the parking lot, no dogs, no car alarms, and he had slept well — at least when he was sleeping.

Wally was bored. Wally hadn't been bored since he invented Kelly Blanton. He should have been, but hadn't been, bored for the entire preceding twenty years. He didn't know what to do about it.

"You wanted to be a writer," Kelly told him. "So, write something."

"Isn't that what you're here for?" Wally asked.

"Not really," Kelly reminded him. "I'm here so that you can get your nerve up and do exciting things. My name will go on the cover. But you and I both know that the writing is up to you."

Wally turned on the tablet and opened the file labeled *Walter Finds a Woman-Tatum.* Skipping down to the end, he found that he really wasn't motivated to write anything. His old writer's guide, however, had mentioned that people who write at least one line a day form good habits. These people tended to be more successful.

The Writer

Walter wrote, somewhat pathetically.

> The dinner was a grand success. Tatum turned out to be a good cook and the cheese had been put to good use. Walter didn't expect to see her again but when he was leaving, she asked if he would like to get together from time to time as friends.

That was all he had. Walter turned off the tablet and spent the next several hours reading the mystery novel that he had bought yesterday. It was good, but Wally needed to get out.

After lunch, he decided that he would go for a ride on his new bike. As he was turning the door knob to leave his apartment, the telephone rang. He wanted to ignore it, but he just wasn't built that way. Wally put his helmet down and picked up the phone.

"Hello," he said with an air of disinterest and distraction.

"Oh." The woman's voice seemed surprised. "I'm sorry. Is this a bad time?"

"That all depends," Wally replied. "If you're calling to sell me something, then, yes, it's a bad time. If you're calling to tell me I won the lottery, then you're fine."

"Neither?" the voice said.

"Go ahead. I've got a minute," Wally said with resignation.

"This is Jacqueline," the voice said.

The Writer

"I'm sorry." Wally felt bad about being rude to a wrong number. "I don't know anyone by that name. You must have the wrong number."

"Maybe." She faltered. "Is this Walter Fleegle?" She paused. "The writer?"

Wally's mind raced. Was this a call back from a publisher? Before he could answer, the voice added, "The biker in the bookstore?"

It was Blondie.

"You couldn't possibly have finished digesting that writer's manual already." He let her know that he had connected the voice to their meeting.

"Oh. No." She laughed. "I haven't. But I was sort of bored today and remembered that you said something about owning a gun. This is very forward of me, I know, but if you're not busy, could you teach me to shoot sometime?"

Wally shrugged. "I suppose." He looked at his watch. "It's just one o'clock now so the range is open. I guess that'd be alright. The truth is that I was sort of bored today too."

"Now?" Jacqueline was startled.

"Or later," Wally replied. "I guess that part would be up to you."

"You're not doing anything?" Jacqueline asked. "I don't want to interrupt."

"No," Wally explained. "Like I said, I was bored too and was just going out for a ride. I can pick you up and we can go to the range."

The Writer

"Fantastic!" Jacqueline actually giggled like a little girl.

Wally wrote down her address and said he could be there in ten minutes. Before he hung up, he told her what he had learned in motorcycle safety class that had never been an issue when he had a scooter. She was to wear solid shoes, jeans, and something long-sleeved and heavy. She could use his old scooter helmet.

Jacqueline was sitting on the front steps with her chin in her hands. She watched him pull into the parking lot, perking up when she recognized who it was. He got the impression that she was like a little kid waiting for the ice cream truck to come by. Except she wasn't little and she wasn't a kid. She'd done as he'd asked and wore calf-high boots over a tight pair of what the young kids called *skinny jeans*. The form fitting fabric had the effect of covering her legs without actually hiding anything. Wally rolled his Triumph up and stopped. Jacqueline greeted him with a broad grin and bounced up from her perch. "Hi there!" she bubbled, her curls bouncing in synch with her steps as she came over.

"Nice jacket," Wally said, complimenting her choice of heavy denim. "Here. Take this helmet and let's get your noggin protected." Putting it on, he noticed how green her eyes were. It must have been dark in the bookstore for him to have missed them before. In the sunshine, they were nothing short of gemstones. Without thinking, be blurted out. "Wow. What great eyes. You're not wearing contacts, are you?"

"Nope." Jacqueline beamed. "All natural. Just like the rest of it."

Wally thought that her statement was a bit odd, but since it could be interpreted two ways, he decided that she meant that she

The Writer

was into organic food. He liked the way the helmet turned her curls into a halo. Maybe she was an angel.

"Jacqueline, huh?" he asked.

Nodding, she confirmed her name adding, "Jacqueline Tait. But call me Jackie, okay?"

"Ready?" he asked. Wally straddled the bike, flipped down the foot pegs for her and waited while she mounted the bike behind him.

"How do you want me?" Jackie asked as she slid her thighs up tight against his hips.

Several different positions came to Wally's mind, but he once again considered the innuendo to be accidental. "Just put your arms around my waist. Lean when I lean. Otherwise just sit there." Wally pushed the starter and the 850cc engine purred to life. Wally was not one for loud bikes and had purchased the best muffler that was available.

Jackie slipped her arms around Walter's waist causing him to cringe slightly as he thought she would think him to be frail. Instead, she gave him a little hug and said, "I think I'm going to like this."

"The ride?" Wally asked.

"That and my new friend," she answered.

Wally put the bike into gear and pulled out into the street. When he did, Jackie leaned up against his back, putting her head almost on his shoulder. Her hands slid up, and crossed so that she was holding his chest with her arms making an X. It was very much like a hug.

The Writer

"Nervous?" he asked.

"Oh, my, no!" she said, squeezing him slightly. "Just the opposite. This is very comfortable. Are you okay? Am I doing this wrong?"

Wally grinned. "I don't think so." He liked the way she was holding him so much that he took the long way to the range. Eventually, though, they arrived and she had to let him go.

Mark was working behind the counter and he recognized Walter right away.

"Hey, buddy." He waved. "What's goin' on? You like that piece I sold you?"

Wally greeted Mark with a smile and introduced Jackie. "Can we share a lane?" Wally asked.

"So, you're an instructor already?" Mark teased. He pointed at Wally, but looked at Jackie. "Are you sure you can trust this guy?"

Jackie didn't answer Mark. She locked her green eyes onto Wally's and said softly, "I think so." Pulling herself back from the moment, she asked Mark, "Why? Do you know something I don't?"

Mark laughed. "Not at all. I'm just ribbin' my buddy here. Sure you can share a lane. Just fill out these waivers and go right in."

When the paperwork had been completed, Wally took Jackie into the ante-room of the indoor range. They both took off their jackets and laid them on a counter. Once again Walter noticed how nicely proportioned she was. The spaghetti-strap top she wore was not nearly as tight as her skinny jeans, but it fit snugly and was three inches short of covering her midriff.

The Writer

It was relatively quiet there and Wally went over the basic safety rules. When he had finished, he made sure that her earmuffs fit well and that her shooting glasses were adjusted properly. Then he took her inside and chose a position on the shooting line. There were eight lanes and only one other person was shooting, so he had lots of choices. Wally showed her how to hang the target in the clips and send it downrange with the electric pulley. She pushed the button and stopped it at five yards.

Wally showed her how to hold the pistol, making sure that she followed all the safety rules. When she fired her first shot and completely missed the target, he had her put it down. From his back pocket, he produced a shooters guide. It was only four pages, but it showed how to aim a pistol using drawings of the sights. She nodded and he told her to try again. Wally decided that she was holding the gun wrong and adjusted her stance.

"Spread your feet apart." he hollered over the gunfire of the other shooter.

"It's a little soon in our relationship for that, isn't it?" She grinned impishly and moved her feet a little further apart. It was the grin this time that made Wally ignore the innuendo. She was playing with him. She was pretty and she knew it. He was somewhat less than handsome and he knew it. She had to be teasing.

"I suppose that depends on your moral code," he hollered back. "Now let me show you how to hold the gun."

Wally stood behind her and reached one arm around either side, putting his hands over hers. He showed her where to put her hands and how to hold the gun steady, then loosened his grip

The Writer

slightly so that she could shoot. She aimed, pulled the trigger, and cursed.

"Damn!" Jackie frowned. "I missed again!"

"You're just not comfortable yet," Wally assured her. He had her pull the trigger without putting a round in the chamber. When she did the muzzle jumped all over the place. Pointing to it, he said, "See? You're not holding it steady. You're anticipating the shot and jumping, causing you to miss."

After a few dozen tries, Jackie was finally able to hit the target regularly. So Wally moved it out to ten yards. After an hour and a half of shooting, Jackie was able to hit the target every time even when it was at fifteen yards. She seldom hit the center, but she hit it.

Later on, out in the parking lot, putting on their jackets and helmets, Jackie looked into Wally's eyes and bubbled like a schoolgirl.

"That was fun!" she said. "What should we do now?"

"What do you want to do?" Wally was fishing for a reason to stay with her. "It's almost four; too early for us to get dinner."

"And too early to go home." Jackie's eyes twinkled while she thought. "Ice cream!" she said elated with her own idea. "We're going to get some ice cream!"

Wally was having a good day and didn't want to end it or be a wet blanket, so he agreed. She snuggled up behind him on the bike again, wrapped her arms around him, and they took off to find the Dairy Magic.

The Writer

They spent the next two hours eating ice cream, talking and riding aimlessly around town. Finally, though, Jackie said that she needed to go home. She had to work the next day and needed to do some laundry first. Walter agreed. He had to work the next day as well.

At her apartment, she climbed off the bike and removed her helmet. Handing it to him, she caught his gaze and said, "We should do something else next weekend You think of something and I'll do it." Without waiting for an answer, she turned and bounced back into her apartment, shouting over her shoulder, "Pick me up at 8 on Saturday morning!"

The Writer

CHAPTER NINETEEN

A STRESSFUL WEEK

Monday morning started out well for Walter Fleegle. The pleasant undercurrents in his emotions that had begun yesterday with Jackie were still flowing through his soul. The morning traffic at the toll booth was light, but interesting. He made change for the standard crowd of commuters, some of whom he saw every day. The daily additions to his character notes were becoming fewer and fewer. The most interesting traveler to pass the booth came somewhat late in the day, but she was a character that needed no enhancement.

The red vintage Firebird had pulled up to the window while Wally was organizing his cash drawer. Sometimes it got a bit messy when traffic was heavy and Wally was sorting things out after the rush had passed. When he turned around to look at the driver, he almost laughed. Maybe he was supposed to. The woman driving was wearing an outfit that made her look like a cross between Wonder Woman and a party clown. Walter guessed that it was probably for an adult party. Her one piece cherry-red bathing suit style outfit was trimmed in gold and had gold lightning bolts originating at the point of each breast and converging at her crotch. Her gold boots, with red trim, rose to just below the knee. A bright blue cape, also with gold trim, was slung about her shoulders. From the neck down, she was gorgeous and provocative. From the neck

185

The Writer

up, she was in full clown face: fuzz ball blue hair, black highlights around her eyes, and a big red squishy nose.

Wally managed to keep a straight face, but after she left, he took out his tablet to make notes. Since there were no other cars approaching, he started goofing around. Jack had told him that it was alright, so Wally decided to take advantage of his kindness. Almost accidentally, he came across his fantasy story about himself and Tatum: *Walter Finds a Woman-Tatum*. Clicking open the file, he refreshed his memory of the story in speed-reading fashion. He had stopped writing last time in a snit of repressed creativity, adding only that Tatum had *asked if he would like to get together from time to time as friends.*

Perhaps it was that current of comfort that cruised through his soul that made him do it, but Wally added a few more lines.

> Tatum spent some time with her new friend (me) and eventually tells him that she loves him. [Note to author – this is not good text. These are outline notes.] There should be dates and stuff, then get engaged. It's okay to sleep with Tatum, but not before I decide that I love her too.

A horn honked, bringing Wally back to his job. "Sorry about that, sir."

Wally made change for the man in the pickup truck, turned off the tablet, and spent the rest of the afternoon focused on the job. He had no plans for the evening and he could write more later.

The Writer

"You mean I can," Kelly interrupted.

"No," Wally snorted. "I mean me. You wrote *Ice*. Actually, you still need to finish that, don't you?"

Kelly acknowledged that he still had no idea about how to get Eddie into the ice coffin in the first place.

"While you're working on that, I'm going to keep up with my fantasy." Wally smiled.

Unfortunately, when he got home and checked his email, he found that he was no longer in the mood to write anything. There were two more rejections. The rejections kept coming all week long and by Friday morning the only thing that kept Wally from throwing Kelly off of a bridge was their date with Jackie on Saturday. As soon as he had that thought, he retracted it, asking himself if this was a date or more time with his new friend. After a while, he decided that it didn't matter what he called it ahead of time. He'd know for sure, one way or the other, when they said goodnight.

That was when the panic set in. He realized that she had said to pick her up Saturday *morning* at eight, not Saturday night. It was up to him to figure out what to do all day and he didn't have much time.

Holy shit! he screamed at himself. *What was he going to do?*

Wally spent his Friday lunch break scouring the internet for ideas. He even called on Kelly for advice. After all, Kelly was the one who had all the confidence and flair. Unfortunately, Kelly was no help at all.

"Uh-uh, dude," Kelly told him. "This is all you. I'm just a writer."

The Writer

Somewhere deep inside, though, Wally knew it wasn't all him. He had invented Kelly and had given him the self-confidence that Wally lacked by giving him the exciting experiences. Both he and Kelly knew that their relationship was changing. It had been Wally, not Kelly who had purchased the Triumph. It was Wally, not Kelly who taught Jackie to shoot. And it would be Wally, not Kelly who planned his Saturday. With that resolved, Walter again searched for ideas on the World Wide Web.

Somehow, by the end of his lunch break, Walter had conquered the demon of indecision and was able to go back to work fully focused on the job.

An hour later, Jackie received a bouquet of carnations with a somewhat lengthy note: *Jacqueline. For tomorrow we have some options. There is a traveling collection of Faberge eggs at the art museum, a book-fair and poetry reading at the Literary Society, and I have coupons for Le Joie de Vivre, if you want to go to dinner.*

Walter's elation at having presented a smorgasbord of possible activities faded into sheer terror by the end of his shift. What if Jackie didn't like art? The exhibit was in one wing of the museum and they could also view a wide variety of paintings and sculpture. Perhaps she might like one of those instead. He knew she was into literature. She worked from home and did say that she was in the field. Mostly he feared his dinner proposal. If she accepted his offer of dinner at an upscale French restaurant, it was definitely going to be a date. The entire evening he stressed about whether he should have suggested something less, and even if he should have suggested dinner at all. Fear played both sides. He feared that she would accept the dinner offer as much as he feared that she wouldn't.

The Writer

By the time he went to bed Friday night, these worries, combined with a week of rejection from publishers and agents, completely disassembled the person that Walter built by proxy through Kelly.

The Writer

CHAPTER TWENTY

COURTSHIP

Saturday morning came suddenly. Somehow, Walter had fallen asleep and had even slept through his alarm. It was the howling of a cat in the parking lot that pulled him to the surface. Peeking at the clock with one eye, he was shocked into full consciousness by the time. It was 7:18. He was going to be late. Fighting back the urge to give in to the constraint, he showered in less than five minutes, shaved in two, skipped coffee, got his jeans and jacket on and flew out the door. Glancing at his watch as he pushed the starter on the Triumph, he realized that he wouldn't even need to speed to get to Jackie's place on time. He just needed to catch the lights.

Jackie was waiting on the steps of her apartment pointing at her watch as Wally rolled up. When he had put the kickstand down and turned the key to quiet the bike, he pulled back the sleeve of his jacket to look at his watch. Sure enough, it was two minutes after eight.

"I'm so sorry!" He grinned, and dismounted.

Jackie had her skinny jeans on again, but this time her blouse was loose fitting and flowing. She was smiling broadly as she thanked him for the flowers.

"I was wondering if you had forgotten." She blinked at him.

The Writer

"Oh, far from it!" Wally exclaimed, remembering his angst.

"Why the flowers?" She grinned. "Why didn't you call?"

"I don't have your phone number," Walter explained.

Jackie laughed. "Caller ID? You didn't save my number after I called you?"

"No." Walter almost blushed. "I didn't know if we would become friends. I don't save numbers unless I have permission. It's a gentleman's way."

She had to admit that he was right about that. On more than one occasion, a man whom she had done business with had used the caller ID to pursue her on a more personal level.

"Well, Walter Fleegle," she said, "you are that. You certainly are a gentleman."

"So, what did you want to do?" Walter raised his eyebrows. "What did you pick?"

Jackie looked surprised, and put her hand to her chest. "I was supposed to pick? I thought we were doing all of those things!"

Walter beamed. Spending the entire day and into the evening with Jackie would be in complete contradiction to his fears of yesterday.

"We can do that." He nodded. "We'll just want to change clothes before we go to dinner. They have a dress code."

Jackie bobbed happily. "Let's go see some eggs!"

Wally flipped down the rear footrest, straddled the bike, and once again took undue pleasure in the way Jackie's legs pressed snugly against his own.

The Writer

"Take the long way to the museum," she suggested. "I like the ride."

Wally did as he was told and managed to spend 25 minutes making the four minute trip from Jackie's apartment to the museum.

Their time at the museum was pleasant and quiet. Admiring the collection of eggs took almost two hours. Jackie was interested in every story that each egg had to tell. She stopped and read every card that accompanied every egg The cards told who the egg was made for, what year it was made, and sometimes included a history of the egg, if it was worth telling. Some of the eggs had survived the conflict of war, being captured, passed around, recaptured and eventually repatriated if not returned to the original owner. Others had traveled the world as gifts from one head of state to another. A few, not many, had been buried in the collections of other museums and in private collections until the organizers of the exhibit had exhumed them.

Each of them was a remarkable work of art. Jackie studied them all.

"That was well worth the ticket!" Jackie said as they completed the tour. "Now let's go see the sculptures. I like sculpture best."

Wally agreed. He too preferred sculpture over painting. The museum wasn't quite world class and was not able to afford many original sculptures, and certainly not the more famous works. It had started as a local museum funded for educational purposes. The result was that the collection included copies of famous works by Rodin, Da Vinci, and Michelangelo as well as originals of lesser work by these same men. The best collection of original work was three pieces by Frederic Remington. Of course there were copies of his

The Writer

other works as well. One hall was still reserved for works by local artists and another for work by local high school students. The exhibits of paintings followed the same pattern. These standing collections were augmented by the traveling exhibits. All in all, the museum had grown into a treasured cultural resource.

Throughout the morning, Walter had not only noticed the eggs and the sculptures, but had also been watching the other people at the museum. This had become habit as he continued to collect characters from wherever they presented themselves. On this particular morning, though, as he observed others, he frequently saw others observing Jackie. It was a new and exciting feeling for Walter Fleegle to be with the girl whom everyone else was admiring. To be honest with himself, he admitted that on more than one occasion, he too had admired the way she filled out her skinny jeans.

"Ready to go?" he asked.

"Can we get lunch before we go to the book fair?" She pouted out the question. "My tummy's rumbling."

Walter took Jackie to a pleasant little Greek restaurant where they shared laughs and a single beer. Wally limited them to one drink because they were on the bike. Jackie was much too sophisticated to act silly in the museum, but at lunch she let loose with a number of observations that had never occurred to Wally.

"That Rodin guy did a lot of sculpting of couples: naked couples, sensuous, attractive naked couples."

"Yeah?" Wally wondered where this was going.

"Do you think they had a problem not getting aroused while he was sculpting? I mean that one, *The Kiss*, they're all over each

The Writer

other. And for *Eternal Idol*, the guy's head is buried between the woman's breasts." Jackie grinned impishly. "It just seems like there may have been problems."

Walter chuckled, but before he could reply, she added, "And what about the grape leaves? Do sculptors imagine those or did the models tie leaves to their junk?"

Walter laughed again.

Jackie touched his hand. "At least Michelangelo got it right. He's got David all raw." She winked at him. "I liked that one."

"Why don't we go to the book fair?" Walter suggested, still struggling to sort out the mad mixture of teasing, innuendo, implication, inference, and insecurity that raged inside him.

Jackie finished her beer and Wally paid the bill. The Literary Society was holding the book fair in a mom and pop bookstore that had a layout designed specifically to accommodate tables for authors. The building was only three minutes from the museum, but once again, Walter managed to stretch the ride significantly. He liked the way Jackie held him close and snuggled tightly behind him. It was funny, he thought, that Jackie was wondering if Rodin's models got aroused. Wally was wondering if he was going to get aroused. While his mind fantasized, his glands were so frightened by these new sensations that they had completely shut down. Without the testosterone, he needn't worry about arousal.

Their walk through the book fair was almost solemn. Both of them loved to read and both of them loved more than just the story. They loved the way that books felt in their hands; the way they smelled, and the way they looked lined up on shelves.

The Writer

"You know?" Jackie mused as she flipped through the pages of the latest romance novel from Jacques DePuis. "I can read a book, put it on the shelf, and every time I walk by and see it there, I relive the entire plot almost instantaneously."

"I do know!" Wally replied. "I do the same thing!"

They walked quietly from table to table as if they were in a library. Jackie seemed to be drawn to mysteries while Wally would pick up anything. Neither of them made a purchase. Jackie touched Wally's arm as he picked up a new cookbook.

"You seem to have very broad interests. Do you actually read that many different kinds of books?"

"I didn't used to," Wally replied. "I was all into mystery and spy thrillers for quite a while, but lately, I want to see what interests other people."

"You're doing research." She gave his arm a gentle squeeze.

"Pretty much," he admitted.

The two bibliophiles wandered slowly and carefully, making sure to visit every single table. When they got to the end of the line, Wally turned towards her.

"Did you see anything that you want to go back and get? Or are we done?"

Jackie stood right in front of Wally and took both of his arms by the elbows. She looked directly into his eyes. It was only slightly uncomfortable for her – she was trying to look sexy, inviting, vulnerable, and submissive, but she was still three inches taller than he was and achieving her goal was difficult while looking *down* into his eyes. Still, she whispered her line softly and with a smile.

The Writer

"I want to read one of *your* books, Mr. Fleegle."

Wally didn't seem to notice the inequality in their stature. What he did notice was that she was sexy, inviting, vulnerable, and submissive. He also noticed that Kelly was whispering in his ear.

"I haven't figured out how to get Eddie into the ice yet!"

"Maybe someday." Wally smiled a crooked smile at Jackie. The best that I've got isn't really ready yet.

As they walked out of the bookstore to the bike, Jackie prodded him for something more.

"Do you have some unfinished work? Perhaps some writing samples? Drafts? I see that sort of thing all the time in my business. I'd really like to see what you've got."

Wally considered showing her some of the summaries he had prepared, but he was afraid. They weren't polished at all. He hadn't even gone back to check for spelling and grammar.

Throwing a leg over his bike, and falling into the seat, he said, "I'm nervous. I've never shown my work to anyone: not a single person." He stopped and corrected himself. "Well, I did send something, just a partial, out to publishers, but I haven't had an acceptance." Wally held out a hand to steady Jackie as she climbed on behind him. "Wait. Do publishers count as people?"

Jackie laughed. "Mostly, no," she agreed.

"You still up for dinner?" he asked as he pushed the starter and revved the engine.

"You bet!" Jackie's enthusiasm was unexpected, but pleasant to hear.

The Writer

"I'll drop you off, go get changed myself, and come pick you up in a taxi." Wally pulled into traffic and made his way to her apartment.

"It's a plan," she snuggled up against him.

At home, Wally made the mistake of checking the mail and found yet another rejection. That made 79. He put it out of his mind and put on his best suit.

When he returned, Jackie was not waiting outside, so he asked the cabbie to wait. Wally tapped somewhat furtively on the door of Jackie's apartment. There was no response. There was no sound coming from inside. Wally's insecurities welled up inside him like the steam in Old Faithful getting ready to blow. He wondered if she had snuck out the back. *Had she stood him up?* She seemed to enjoy the day, but maybe the actual *date* part of the day had been too much for her. He tapped again, only slightly more loudly.

Walter Fleegle waited. The cabbie waited. They exchanged glances. It was clear to Wally that the cabbie thought he had been stood up too.

Then the door creaked and opened slightly. A pair of flashy green eyes and a pouty face, framed in tight little blonde curls, peeked out at him. "I'm not sure about this, Wally."

Walter's heart sank. He knew that the day, the relationship so far, had been too good to be true. He tried to tear himself away from those captivating eyes and leave.

Jackie opened the door a little more.

"I can't decide what to wear. I want to look perfect for you tonight." For a second, Wally thought she was going to start sobbing. "I just can't seem to get this right."

The Writer

"Let me see," Wally said and gently pushed the door all the way open. As he did so, Jackie took two steps back. She was still wearing her pouty face, but Wally wasn't looking at her face. Jackie had put on an emerald green, snug fitting dinner dress. The cut accentuated her breasts, her hips and her thighs, which is where it ended: half way to her knees. The top was off-the-shoulder with a deeply cut neckline which only served to enhance her natural proportions. Unlikely as it might have seemed, the dress was complemented by black pumps, a black belt, and a black choker studded with a single large pearl. Finally, Wally's eyes drifted to her face. Her hair, still in tight blonde curls, was perfect, her makeup, which was minimal, was perfect and her green eyes were sad.

Wally looked at her for an inappropriately long period of time and finally announced, "I see what's wrong." Stepping close to her, he adjusted one curl on her left temple, took a step back and beamed.

"There. Now it's perfect. You're perfect."

His bit of play-acting seemed to satisfy Jackie and she giggled, bouncing on her heels as she did. That display of happiness sent a jiggle through her curls. It was a jiggle that rippled down her body as if a rock had been tossed in a pond.

"You look beautiful," Wally said with admiration. "The taxi is waiting. Would you care to join me?"

Wally cocked his arm out to the side. Jackie took it and they ambled to the taxi as if they had all night to get there. Wally assured himself that, yes, this was a date and that Jackie had made no mistake about it at all. Hopefully, he could keep himself from making any mistakes for the next few hours. *That would be good*, he told himself. Kelly was quick to agree.

The Writer

Le Joie de Vivre lived up to its name. For a French restaurant, it was surprisingly welcoming – *not stiff* might be a better term. The décor was certainly upscale, and there was a dress code, but there was no haughtiness associated with the staff or the guests. It was comfortable. Wally, of course, was taking mental notes in case Kelly needed to describe it in a future book. Wood paneled walls were decorated with coats of arms, crossed swords, and photographs of the French countryside; vineyards, cattle grazing in lush green fields, an old man in coveralls walking a pig on a leash, and what looked like it might have been a cheese factory.

Jackie turned quite a few heads as they were shown to their table – a table covered with a heavy black cotton cloth. It wasn't the standard thin table cloth that you might find at a lesser restaurant. It was as thick as the cloth dinner napkin – which was also black. The pure white china plates and alabaster drinking glasses provided a very stark contrast. The floor was highly polished wood, into which were inlaid replicas of famous French woodcarvings and scenery. Decorative scrollwork was filled in with what looked like gold, and coated with a hard lacquer. They were literally walking on art.

Dinner began, of course, with a glass of wine. Malbec or Shiraz? That was the question that Jackie was hung up on. The waiter, quite aware of the uneducated palate of most Americans, brought out a small glass of each, a large glass of water, and two soda crackers. Jackie sipped one, ate the crackers, drank the water, and sipped the other.

"They're both so good!" she whispered to Wally. "Which do you like?"

The Writer

"Leave them both," Wally said to the waiter. "We'll figure it out as we go."

"Comme tu veux," he said and retreated.

"Do you know French?" Jackie was incredulous.

"Not at all." Wally laughed. "But the waiter left both bottles, so I guess he said *okay!*" Wally poured a glass of wine for each of them.

"Haven't you ever been here before?"

"No!" Jackie was surprised by the question. "Why would you think that?"

While Wally was wondering why he thought *that*, Jackie added, "I couldn't afford something like this on what I make. Have you been here?"

Kelly whispered in Wally's ear, "Girls like Jackie never pay for dinner."

"Go away," Wally told him. "I need to answer her question." Wally smiled at Jackie wondering if she could tell that he was holding two conversations at once.

"No." He laughed. "I've never been here. I'm a toll booth attendant, remember?"

"How did you pick this place, then? How can you afford it?" Jackie sipped her wine and looked at him inquisitively.

"I've saved a little money over the years waiting for the right time to spend it." He raised his glass and touched it to hers. "This seemed like the right time."

The Writer

"Good job!" Kelly interrupted. Wally had to tell him to get lost, again.

"I found the place in the weekend magazine." Wally looked around the room. "I suppose it'll do. I kind of need a little boost anyway; a good dinner, a little wine, and the pleasure of your company might do the trick."

"I thought things were going well." Jackie looked concerned. "We had a great day and now … well … we can have a great night if someone doesn't get himself all in the dumps."

Reaching across the table, she put her hand on his. "Did something happen?"

"I got another rejection." Wally swirled his wine in his glass, staring into the little whirlpool it made, he thought that his life was doing the same thing.

"Get a grip," Kelly interjected again. "You're here with a beautiful woman drinking expensive wine. Remember what you said about fast cars and faster women? Well, Jackie isn't exactly fast, but if you get her drunk enough, you might get some tonight. We need that experience to write about it, remember?"

"Not this time, Kelly. Not with this woman." Wally rejected Kelly.

"That's too bad," Jackie was saying while Wally dealt with his alter ego.

Wally looked up from the swirling red liquid, determined to get the better of his emotions. "Maybe not."

"What do you mean?" Jackie asked earnestly.

The Writer

"Remember earlier when I said that I was unsure about letting you read any of my work?" Jackie nodded. "Well, the rejection turned out to be the leverage I needed to break out of my shell. I brought a few things with me."

Jackie was ecstatic. "What did you bring me? Let me see?" Her little curls bounced with enthusiasm and her green eyes almost exploded with eagerness.

Walter pulled a folded piece of paper out of his jacket pocket.

"It's just a summary: a plot summary. I wanted to start small." He handed her the summary about the race car driver whose wife was plotting to kill him for sleeping with the test driver's girlfriend.

Jackie read through it quickly, sipping her wine as she did.

"This is a good plot line. Are you going to work it up into a story?"

"I think I want to finish *Ice* first. I'd like to get it published," Walter said.

"Well, you've got some time on your hands while you wait for the next rejection letter." Jackie attempted to lighten the mood. Walter obliged her with a smile, even if it was a sad smile.

"What else did you bring me?"

"Nothing," Wally admitted. When he saw how crestfallen Jackie looked, he determined to do something. Walter waved to the waiter. One of the things that Walter had liked about the review in the weekend paper was that the waiters didn't hound you for your dinner order. People could sit and talk for hours before placing an order or they might never place an order at all. When the waiter arrived, Walter asked if he had a tablet that he might

The Writer

borrow and if the restaurant had wi-fi. The waiter was confused, but didn't show it. He spoke softly.

"Oui, monsieur."

"I think I can get you something from my cloud account." Wally's smile was met with a happy grin from Jackie. A few moments later, the waiter returned with a tablet and the password. Walter logged into his account and pulled up his story about the hang gliding accident. Jackie read it with real interest.

"This is actually a pretty good setup." She nodded. "Where are you going to take the story from there?"

"It can go anywhere," Wally said. "I could have any one of the characters be the good guy. All I really did was to introduce some characters."

"Right." Jackie nodded. "Did you have something in mind?"

"I got stuck deciding if the woman who was rescued would be a nun, a minister, or the love interest of the instructor who saved her," Walter explained.

"That makes sense." Jackie tossed her head from side to side, considering the alternatives and bouncing her curls.

"Are you working on it?"

"Not really," Walter confessed. "I'm having my doubts that this is the right thing for me at all. I thought that with 87 queries, I might get something. Even a response that indicated that something might be possible is better than nothing."

"You've still got some queries out there." Jackie took his hand again. "In this business, you have to be patient and persistent." She bounced her curls again. "Or you self-publish."

The Writer

"I might have to," Wally conceded.

"How much money do you have?" Jackie blushed. "I mean to spend on publishing and promoting." She tapped his hand. "I didn't mean to pry."

"I could afford it, I suppose," Walter admitted. "I don't want to have to do that, though. I want to get published because my work is good, not because I can buy it."

"I understand." Jackie filled their wine glasses. "But you're setting a bar for yourself that almost no one reaches."

Jackie took a long hard look at Walter.

"Look. You have talent. I can see that. Remember, I work in this field doing editorial crap. I've seen it all. You can do this, but you have to get people's attention. You have to buy that attention or you have to already be famous for something else. That's the way it works."

"Are you sure?" Wally was encouraged.

"Absolutely." Jackie pointed at the tablet. "I'll prove it to you. Write something right now."

Walter was stunned and afraid. He wanted to refuse, but she had captured him again with her stare. Wally thought that she must be the female version of the Green Lantern, using her eyes as her power source. With that, he also realized that he does have the imagination to come up with random thoughts that could be a whole book. He could write not only a novella but a series based on nothing more than the Green Lantern-ness sitting across the table. But he'd need a better name for her.

The Writer

<u>Paper Tiger - by Walter Fleegle</u>

Sammy Smith had turned 14 the day before school let out for the summer. Sammy Smith needed a job. Fortunately, his cousin worked as a delivery man for the Detroit Morning News and had been able to get Sammy assigned to a paper route on the east side. That was three days ago.

An old big frame bicycle was all Sammy had for transportation. He had attached a plastic milk crate to the top of the rear fender and two more to each side of the rear wheel. With another one positioned on the front handle bars, he was able to carry all the papers for his route at one time. He didn't mind the early start of the day, but pedalling his route had made his legs sore. Sammy figured that he'd get used to it by the end of the week and so just willed himself through the stiffness and pain. That's the way Sammy was.

A dense fog had settled over the city during the night and Sammy found himself pedaling down 4th Street without being able to see more than 15 yards ahead. He'd really need to pay attention to make sure he didn't miss a delivery. The fog was thick enough that it made his face wet as he pedaled along. He could feel the tiny droplets hit him on his cheeks and forehead when he pedaled fast enough. Sammy worried that it would ruin the papers. The people in the warehouse hadn't thought to put them into plastic

The Writer

sleeves because when they loaded the papers into lots for delivery, it hadn't been raining.

Sammy completed one route in a small neighborhood and headed to his next cluster of deliveries. He had to cross 1st to get there. No one lived on 1st. Instead, there were rows of small shops; rundown shops, for the most part. There was only one that took the paper and he pedaled towards it. After he dropped that single paper, he would head into the other neighborhood.

Racing past the little shop, he flipped the paper up against the front door and turned the corner at the end of the building. Sammy had taken the corner a little too fast and was unable to stop or maneuver to avoid hitting the couple who had appeared before him. Sammy slammed into the man and the woman screamed. Papers, the bike, Sammy, and the man scattered out onto the pavement. The woman screamed. Both Sammy and the man got up and Sammy began to apologize to him. The woman screamed. That's when Sammy began to re-evaluate the situation.

The man struck Sammy across the face, knocking him back to the ground. Sammy hit the pavement hard, rolled onto his back and yelled at the man, "Dude! I said I was sorry!"

The Writer

The woman screamed. Sammy noticed that the man was holding a purse. The woman's blouse was torn, and the woman was still screaming. *What have I stumbled onto?* Sammy asked himself. Part of his answer was being delivered by the man who had come over to where Sammy was and had started to kick him. As he delivered a kick, Sammy crossed his arms at the wrist, palms facing inward, and caught his leg just above the ankle. The woman screamed as Sammy slid his hands down to the man's foot, adjusted his grip, and twisted the man's entire leg, using his foot as leverage. The man fell down, and the woman screamed.

Sammy picked up two rolled up newspapers from the street and began to pummel the man with them. All Sammy really had for weapons were his speed and reflexes. The papers wouldn't really hurt the man, but they would confuse him and distract him. The man dodged and ducked and protected his face while Sammy landed insignificant blow after insignificant blow. Like most criminals, at heart, this one too was just a coward. Finally he dropped the purse and ran off. The woman screamed.

Sammy retrieved her purse and started apologizing again. Only then did he notice that the reason she had not run away, but had stood there screaming, was because she was blind. He found her red and white cane against the wall and handed it to her. "Ma'am,"

The Writer

he calmed her. "It's alright now. The mugger is gone."

The police car pulled up and two officers jumped out, guns drawn and hollering at Sammy.

"Put the purse down!"

"Put your hands up!"

"On the ground! NOW!"

Sammy did as he was told, realizing that there were no witnesses to vouch for him. The evidence provided by his bicycle and newspapers would not exonerate him.

Walter Fleegle ended his little story and handed the tablet to Jackie.

She had watched him intently as he had written and now he watched her as she read. From the look on her face, she was impressed, but not ecstatic. Jackie put the tablet down and sipped her wine.

"I was right." She tapped the tablet with her finger. "You've got talent. You just need some practice and some polish."

"How can you tell?" Wally asked. "Was it the sentence structure, the style, the setup? What'd you like?"

Jackie shrugged. "Those are the technical things. What makes it work is that at the end of your last paragraph, I found myself wanting to know what happens to Sammy next. Is he wrongfully incarcerated? Does the woman turn out to be a wealthy spinster?

The Writer

Maybe she's the last in her family tree and she gives him her estate when she dies? The story could be about how he deals with going from East Detroit poverty to being a millionaire. Or the story could instill in Sammy the desire to become a policeman." Her eyes once again held his. "I want to know what Wally will have him do. That's what makes it good."

Walter nodded. "I don't know. You might be saying that to be nice."

The formerly friendly green eyes flashed like a death ray.

"Don't insult me. Don't insult yourself." She softened. "You need to do this."

"She's right, you know," Kelly interrupted.

"Go home!" Wally ejected Kelly once again.

The rest of the dinner was quiet, comfortable and amazing. The food was amazing, she was amazing, the fact that she believed in him was amazing. Standing outside her apartment door, Wally started to become nervous once again. *What if she asks me in?* he thought. *What if she doesn't?* he countered. Jackie turned to face him and looked down at him.

"You go home and write. I'll see you next Saturday and I want to see progress."

Jackie put her hand on Wally's shoulder and leaned over, giving him a gentle kiss on the cheek.

The Writer

CHAPTER TWENTY-ONE

COINCIDENCE

Monday morning came all too soon for Walter Fleegle. He had spent three hours on Sunday at the pistol range and then test drove the Alpha Romeo again. Jackie had wanted to get together and do something, but he was afraid. He wanted – no, he needed – to be alone and try to come to grips with what was happening. His whole life seemed to be changing. The alter-ego that he had created had awakened something in Wally that was unfamiliar. After 20 or so years of celibacy, Walter Fleegle almost had a girlfriend. He was doing exciting things. He had money. He was writing. Jackie said he was good. He'd written an off-the-cuff story for her last night, and she said it was good. Wally was reading his story about Sammy to see if he could see what she had seen.

"Careful with that," Kelly teased. "You want to keep some of it, don't you?"

"Shut up," Wally said, realizing that he had changed. He was now rejecting Kelly's dominance. Wally wanted Kelly to stay where he belonged: on the cover.

"Sure," Kelly continued and Wally flopped into his understuffed chair with the morning paper, "but before I go, look at that news item at the bottom of page one."

Wally read the article just to make Kelly go away. Kelly didn't.

210

The Writer

"See? An 18 year old girl delivering pizza to an old lady interrupted a home invasion," Kelly told Wally the meat of the story before he had a chance to read it.

Wally read the story.

The young woman arrived shortly after a man had broken into a house owned by an elderly single woman who was confined to a wheelchair. The door was still open, so when she got to it, she naturally looked inside and hollered, "Pizza! Did someone order pizza?"

When the robber turned to her and she saw his gun, she threw the pizza in his face, and charged him. A hand-slap with her left hand, and a counter-slap with her right, lifted the gun right out of the robber's hand and put it into hers. The reporter offered the opinion that the subsequent kick to the groin and roundhouse kick to his knee, dislocating that joint and sending him to the ground in pain, was probably an excessive use of force. The young woman, a Samantha Goliad, was quoted as being thankful that her parents had put her in karate class when she was six. The years of training and work had been worth it. She also had some unprintable words that she used to describe a man who would rob a woman in a wheelchair.

"So?" Wally snorted. "A real life hero gets her name in the paper. What of it?"

The Writer

"You don't see it, do you?" Kelly shook his head in disbelief. "A handicapped old lady, a delivery, an interrupted robbery, the unlikely hero? Doesn't that sound familiar?"

"I suppose," Wally admitted. "What of it? Robberies happen all the time."

"Sammy? Samantha?" Kelly persisted.

"What are you getting at?" Wally screwed up his face.

"Ya know?" Kelly gave up. "Forget it. If you don't see what's going on, I can't help you."

"I gotta go to work." Wally got up and went to take a shower.

Monday and Tuesday passed in what was becoming Wally's new routine. Every day he collected more character profiles, telling himself that someday they would come in handy. Every evening he would check his email and get one or two more rejections

Wednesday evening, he called Kelly on the carpet.

"Look." Walter was almost angry. "You need to figure out how Eddie got into the ice. If we can't get a publisher or an agent, I've decided to self-publish."

"You're just pissed because of all the rejections," Kelly countered.

"Maybe so, but you still need to finish *Ice*." Walter stood firm.

"If I were you, I'd be more worried about where you're going to take Jackie on Saturday." Kelly deflected, and then redirected, Wally's runaway emotions in order to save himself. He had not thought of anything that made sense and that would put Eddie into his predicament.

212

The Writer

"Shit," Wally muttered. "What am I gonna do?"

"Do what I do," Kelly suggested. "You taught it to me."

"What's that?" Walter was confused.

"Put yourself in the situation and see what you – or a normal person – would do." Kelly laughed. To Kelly it might have been a joke, but to Wally it made perfect sense. Wally got his tablet and settled into his understuffed chair. Finding the file labeled, *Walter Finds a Woman-Tatum,* Wally went to where he had left off and read the last few lines.

"Wow. That's weak." He criticized his last entry. The outline was there – dating, love, getting engaged. What he needed was a date. Titles to his other summaries and outlines were listed in a box on the left side of his screen. One of them caught his eye: *The Cruise*. Wally wouldn't want to take Jackie out on a shipwreck, but day sailing might be fun. Just to see what it looked like in print, Wally typed more to his story.

> Tatum wanted to go sailing. So I took her. We had a really nice time.

"What the fuck is that?" Kelly asked. "You were getting pretty good at this stuff and now it's like you're reverting to … whatever that was when we started."

"I'm just not sure what's going on," Wally admitted.

"You're afraid," Kelly blurted out the truth.

"I've got every right to be afraid," Wally countered.

"Not anymore." Kelly sneered. "I fixed that."

The Writer

When the phone rang and interrupted their argument, Wally threw the tablet at Kelly and ordered him to get to work on *Ice*.

"Hello?" Wally answered the phone in a voice still gruff from his argument with Kelly.

"Hey? Are you okay?" Jackie asked.

Wally softened almost immediately but was still concerned about Saturday. "I'm better now. I was stuck at a difficult spot in something I was writing."

"Well, at least you're writing." Jackie bubbled. "I think that's great. Stuck or not."

"Thanks," Walter almost whispered. "It's nice to have someone to believe in me."

"You're welcome," Jackie replied softly. "You're easy to believe in." Neither of them spoke for a moment.

"Anyway!" Jackie got herself back on track. "The reason I called is because I was sitting here doing a little reading and a thought came to me out of nowhere."

"What's that?" Wally asked.

"Can we go sailing this weekend?"

"See?" Kelly interjected.

"I don't see why not," Wally said. "I'll come get you around nine?"

"That'd be great." Jackie was satisfied. "Should I buy a mask and snorkel or will we just sail?"

The Writer

"As you wish! We can sail out to one of the islands in the bay, snorkel around it, and sail home." Wally was becoming enthusiastic.

"See you Saturday!" Jackie said. "Now get back to writing!"

"Bye." Wally hung up. Turning to Kelly, he said. "You keep working on your story. I'm going to watch TV."

Kelly just shook his head. "You still don't get it."

Wally refused to get drawn into Kelly's fantasy again and ignored him.

The Writer

CHAPTER TWENTY-TWO

A DAY ON THE BAY

Sailing had never been one cf Wally's passions until he took Kelly to St. Thomas. Before the trip, he had read adventure books and sailing manuals in order to prepare Kelly for the experience. When he got back, though, it was Wally who went to the local marina and rented a sailboat for the day. He'd only gone out four or five times, but he was comfortable enough that he wasn't timid about going out with Jackie. What made him uncomfortable was going out with Jackie at all. Wally was worried that today, out on the boat, Jackie would notice his short leg and all his deformities would suddenly be all that she would see.

"Come on, Wally," Kelly encouraged him. "You've made immense progress. Don't lose traction now."

"I'm worried," Wally said. "I've got emotions running around inside me that are very strange: very unusual."

"She likes you, you jerk!" Kelly had been growing impatient with Wally for several weeks. This morning's temerity was pushing him to the edge. "You like her! That's what you're feeling!"

"Okay, okay." Wally pulled to a stop in front of Jackie's apartment. "Don't yell."

The Writer

Jackie must've been watching from the window, because the door opened and she bounded out, curls bouncing, eyes flashing their accent to her happy grin.

"What're you doing?" Wally asked.

Jackie was taken aback. "Aren't you happy to see me?"

"Shorts?" Wally pointed to her Bermuda shorts and shook his head. "Not on my bike. I'd hate to mess up those beautiful legs if I did something stupid."

"Aw." Jackie smiled. "You care about me." It took less than five minutes for her to put on long pants and get her jacket.

"Ready now?" She pulled at her pant-leg. "Do I pass inspection?"

Wally nodded and she hopped on behind him. Leaning up against his back and threading her arms around his chest, she whispered, "Will there be another inspection for proper sailing and swimming attire later?"

Wally just grinned, pushed the starter, and rolled out of the parking lot. The people at the marina were expecting them and their rental was all set to go. Wally had chosen a 24 foot sloop for the day. It was state-of-the-art, too. He could manage almost everything from the cockpit. The sails were all equipped with motor driven winches and roller furlers. All he really had to do was work the rudder and adjust the trim of the sail using the levers on the console. It was unusual for a rental to have all these extras, but Wally had convinced the marina sales department that he was looking for something to buy. Today was the marine version of the Alpha Romeo test drive.

217

The Writer

"Gimme a minute to get squared away here, okay?" Wally pointed to a seat in the cockpit. Jackie dutifully sat down, impressed with his command of the situation and confidence with the boat.

The wind was cooperating this morning, which reduced Wally's stress considerably. He slipped the mooring lines and the wind eased him away from the dock. He was glad that he didn't have to use the outboard for that. It was stinky and he hated the sound of it. As he had grown to like sailing, he had also grown to appreciate the relative peace and quiet that it brought. Wally pressed the right buttons, and the jib unfurled, flapping softly in the light breeze as it did. He took the tension out of the sheet and trimmed the sail to match his heading. He would use the jib to get them out into the bay, then raise the mainsail.

As they sailed out into the bay, Jackie asked if she could go below and look at the rest of the boat. Wally nodded – he was busy avoiding other traffic in the narrow channel and didn't need any distractions at the moment.

Sailboats of this size are equipped with the marine version of a Dutch door. But instead of there being two doors, the top half is a hatch in the cabin roof, while the bottom half is in the wall of the cabin. To open it, Jackie had to slide the hatch forward, then open the bottom part like a regular door. Jackie disappeared below.

Three minutes later, Wally called to Jackie, "We're clear of the channel and can hoist the man now. You wanna come up and watch?"

Jackie appeared in the cabin below, just inside the door. "Can I take off my long pants yet?"

"Oh! Sure! I'm sorry. I just got busy." Wally apologized.

The Writer

Jackie had already removed her riding jacket and Wally could tell that she had come prepared, wearing her swimsuit under her clothing. The almost gossamer white cover-up she wore did little to conceal her black bikini top. Jackie took a seat on one of the cabin benches and removed her riding boots. Wally didn't think that removing footwear could be sexy, but somehow Jackie made it seem so.

"Where should I put these?" She pointed to her boots and socks.

"If you lift up the cushion of that bench you're sitting on, you'll find a hatch. There's a locker underneath. Stick them in there."

"Okay." Jackie stood. "Pants too?"

Wally nodded and watched as Jackie, perhaps a little too slowly, unsnapped her jeans, unzipped them, and slid them down to her ankles. Stepping out of them, she watched Wally watch her, and smiled broadly.

"Do you like this?" She made a motion with her hand that might have meant that she was asking about her bikini but also might have meant that she was asking about her firm breasts, flat stomach, and toned legs.

"I do." Wally grinned.

Jackie bent over, picked up her shoes and jeans, rolling them into a ball as she did. To lift he cushion, she had to turn away from Wally and face the seat. Wally was entranced. Under the cushion, she found the hatch and bent over to open it and put her things away. Once again, Wally thought that maybe she spent a little more time than was needed to do so. Wally spent the extra time well,

The Writer

admiring how well her bikini covered all the most important things and revealed everything that wasn't illegal to show in public.

Jackie closed the hatch, replaced the cushion, and joined Wally in the cockpit.

"Watch this." Wally kept his composure, but it was difficult. Her transparently obvious display of her sexuality had achieved the intended effect and Wally could feel the pressure building inside him. But in his head, he couldn't fight down the conflict between his lust and his emotions. Kelly was right about one thing. Wally wanted her. He wanted her desperately. But Wally was right about what he wanted too. He didn't want another pity piece like the last time he had been with a woman and he didn't want a *thanks for taking me to dinner and sailing* piece. Wally's problem was that he thought he was falling in love with Jackie, but he wasn't quite sure what love was.

She was pretty, smart, congenial, and apparently quite self-sufficient. She was younger than he was but not by so many years that anyone would notice. She loved books and literature – she even had a job doing editing work. Wally didn't know what kind of editing, but the job was consistent with her love of the English language. Just as he had, she had earned her college degree in a low income major just because she liked it. On the other hand, Wally didn't know anything about her family, her past, her politics, or even her religion. Somehow, though, these things didn't seem to matter. If her mother was an alcoholic, an axe murderer, or a shoe salesman, it wouldn't change who Jackie was.

"Watch what?" Jackie brought Wally back to the surface. "You asked me if I wanted to come up and watch, remember?"

The Writer

"Press this button." Wally pointed to the console. In order to reach the button, she had to stand close to Wally, putting an arm around his waist to steady herself against the movement of the boat. *Damn, she smells good.* Wally thought as her curls tickled his cheek. Jackie pressed the button, and an electric winch hummed, reeling in the mainsail halyard, lifting the canvas to the top of the mast.

Wally worked the control that adjusted the sheet to trim the main, and soon they were slipping across the bay at five knots. The boat wanted to glide through the water, but there was just enough chop that it bounced every five or six seconds. Wally liked the way she had kept her arm around his waist, steadying herself with her other hand on the console. She could easily have sat down, but she wanted to be next to him. She was enjoying the ride. He was enjoying her. Wally was very close to convincing himself that he had found love.

They stayed like that all the way across the bay. They didn't talk much. A quiet comfortableness welled up in Wally that only served to reinforce his suspicions about where their relationship was headed.

"Can we go there?" Jackie pointed to a small island in the bay.

"Sure." Wally spun the wheel a quarter turn, and adjusted the sails using the power winch. "What do you have in mind?"

"You said we could snorkel!" Jackie replied. "Did you bring gear?"

Wally smiled. "You didn't mention it again and I was unsure, but I had the marina people put some gear on board anyway. I really wasn't sure if you were serious, but I didn't want to take the chance of screwing up." Wally paused. "I do that a lot."

The Writer

"Walter Fleegle!" Jackie said, putting her finger in his face. "You stop that!" She wiggled it. "In all the time I've known you, you haven't screwed up a thing. Every day has been perfect. Your writing is ... well, I can't lie, it's not perfect, but it can be perfect."

Jackie was fed up. She took Wally's face in her hands and kissed him hard. When her lips parted and her tongue touched Wally's, he had to call it off.

"Hey!" he mumbled through the kiss. "I still have to drive this thing!"

Jackie let him go. "We'll finish this later." Wally wasn't sure if she meant finishing the ass-chewing or the kiss. A few minutes later, he pointed to the bow.

"Can you go up there and throw the anchor over the side when I tell you to?"

Jackie nodded, patted him on the butt, and did her best to make her way forward with a sexy strut – but the rocking of the boat on the waves made it seem like a drunken, but still sexy, stumble instead. At the bow, she collected the anchor and leaned against the rail of the bow pu pit.

"Ready!" she called. "I think."

"Don't step on the line!" Wally hollered. "Keep your feet clear!"

Wally steered into the wind as they got close to the island. When the sails were fully luffed, and flapping in the breeze, Wally engaged the roller furler of the mainsail and motioned for Jackie to drop the anchor. She paid out twenty feet of line before Wally jumped out of the cockpit and ran forward to tie it off.

The Writer

The anchor caught and the wind pushing against the flapping jib helped set it. Wally told Jackie to come aft with him so that she would be clear of the jib when he furled it and they made their way back to the cockpit.

"Push that one." Wally pointed to the console. Jackie pressed the button and furled the jib.

"Well done!" he said.

Jackie smiled at him, her green eyes glowing in the sun, surrounded by her halo of golden curls.

"Now, where were we?" She gathered him to her and kissed him again. This time, she was tender and soft. Wally enjoyed her closeness and how her tongue explored him. The unintended consequence was that his fear rose as rapidly as his heart rate. Wally pulled back slightly.

"Give me time," he said. "Let's go for a swim."

"What's the matter, Wally?" Jackie looked concerned. "I thought you would like this. I thought we were ... getting close."

"We are," he admitted, "but it's been twenty years or so for me and I want to be sure of what I'm doing." In a stupid and instinctive defensive reaction, he added, "How long has it been for you?"

Jackie looked serious. "What does that matter?" She shook her curls. "I'm no saint. But I'm no slut either. I really thought you liked me, Wally."

"I do," he replied. "It's just so very new for me to have someone like me back." In a not-so-stupid recovery, he lodged his

The Writer

plea. "I'm looking forward to your help in getting over that. Will you help me?"

Jackie softened and kissed him gently this time. "Let's go swimming."

Wally and Jackie retrieved the snorkel gear and slid into the water. After swimming the 50 yards to shore, they were disappointed. On the swim, all they had seen was a lot of seagrass and a couple of starfish.

"Let's go explore the island," Jackie suggested.

Wally's fear returned, completely overwhelming the pleasure of the last thirty minutes.

"Okay," he agreed timidly.

"What's the matter?" Jackie stood up in the shallow water and removed her mask. Wally liked the way her suit clung to her when it was wet. Telling himself to stay focused, he stood too.

"I have a problem," he admitted. "You may not have noticed before, but you will now."

"What is it?" Jackie took his hand.

"I have a bit of a limp. I wear a lift in one shoe, so you may not have noticed before, but one of my legs is shorter than the other." Wally was relieved that his secret was out in the open.

For a moment, Jackie couldn't think of what to say. The length of his leg didn't matter, but it was clear that this was an emotional thing for Wally, not a rational one.

"Does that make you walk in circles?" She giggled. "I mean without the lift?"

The Writer

Wally was stunned. Jackie stepped close to him and kissed him again.

"Let me put it another way." She grinned. "I don't give a shit. I'm not dating your leg." She laughed again. "At least not yet!"

Jackie bounced towards shore with her mask and fins in her hand, each bounce drawing Walter's attention to her well rounded ass and away from his deformity. Her gambit was successful and he walked to shore, somewhat off-kilter, after her. He felt much better. She "didn't give a shit" about his damn leg.

The island was small and it didn't take long to explore most of it. Their most interesting, and perplexing, discovery was how many people had left things there. Some of what they found seemed to be debris washed up with the tide, but the blankets, the beach chair, the broken Styrofoam cooler full of empty beer cans, and a variety of condom packages, were obviously left by oblivious and uncaring visitors.

After circling the island, Wally and Jackie sat in the sand near where their boat was anchored. They just sat, made small talk, and then stretched out on the sand to bake in the sun. The afternoon was idyllic, but it had to end.

"I have to pee," Jackie announced, breaking the spell.

"Let's swim back to the boat. You can take care of it along the way." Wally grinned, and lifted himself up on one elbow. "But before we go, I want you to know that I'm quite comfortable with you. You're an amazing woman." Wally touched her hand. "I've been thinking about this all morning now." He paused. "No, actually I've been thinking about this for about two weeks."

Jackie's eyes said *What? What is it Wally?*

The Writer

"I think ... I think I might be in love with you." Jackie beamed, giving Wally courage. "No. That's not quite right. I'm pretty sure that I'm in love with you."

Jackie rolled over onto Wally, pushing him back down flat on his back. She kissed him fully and deeply, pressing her body against his. Pulling back slightly, she brushed his hair with her hand before looking him in the eyes.

"Walter Fleegle," she said, "I've been in love with you ever since you tried to steal my writer's guide."

She kissed him again. His heart was racing. He could feel the beat of her heart against his chest match his own.

"But I still have to pee."

Wally laughed. Jackie laughed with him. The swim back to the boat was a little more exciting than the swim to the island had been. They surprised a school of rays, but they were the kind that didn't have stingers. A flounder bursting out of the sand where he had buried himself startled them as much as they had startled him. By the time they were on board the sail boat, their passion had subsided and they were once again just enjoying each other's company.

"Did you take care of your problem?" Wally asked as he helped Jackie up the ladder and onto the boat.

"All done!" she confessed to her crime of pollution. "But now I have another."

"What?" he asked.

The Writer

"Can we rinse off anywhere?" Jackie pulled on her curls. "The seawater is sticky, and, to be honest, that rolling around in the sand left … um … "

"You have sand in your swimsuit?" Wally grinned.

Jackie nodded.

"All we have is a hose and about fifty gallons of water," Wally said. "There's no shower on board, but I can rinse you off on deck."

Jackie agreed and Wally pulled the hose out of the storage locker beneath a seat in the cockpit. He had Jackie stand on the deck and pushed a button on the console that would pressurize the water system.

"This might be cold," he advised.

"Go ahead." She grimaced.

Walter opened the stopcock at the end of the hose and dribbled water over her head.

"Is that too cold?"

"No. Yes. No. Go ahead." Jackie steeled herself against the shock.

Wally opened the valve wider and Jackie massaged her hair to loosen the sand. When she finished, she took his hand in hers and guided it to her neck.

"Now here." She grinned, wiping her eyes with her other hand. She pulled her suit away from her breast a little and guided the hose down to where the water would wash the sand out from behind her bra. Then she did the other side.

The Writer

"Wally?" Jackie released his hand. "This isn't working." She unhooked her bra and tossed it aside. "Now you can rinse me off properly."

Wally did as he was told with a mixture of admiration and lust. He wanted to touch her. He wanted to kiss her. He was still afraid.

"Okay," she said. "Now the bottoms." Jackie removed her bikini and turned away. "Rinse my ass first, please." Wally applied the stream of water as directed.

"It's cold, isn't it?" He streamed water between her cheeks to wash the sand out. "You have goosebumps on your ass."

"Now the front." Jackie turned to face him. "Do a good job."

Wally aimed the stream of water onto the tuft of blonde hair that proved she was not a bleach-blond.

"Wow," he exclaimed.

"Do you like that?" Jackie asked.

"Yes, I do, but I was referring to how much sand got in there." Wally laughed.

Jackie brushed her fingers through the hair.

"I think that's got it." Taking the hose from his hand, she grinned and said, "Your turn." Jackie pulled the drawstring on Wally's swim trunks and let them fall to the deck.

"What about my hair?" He asked. "Up here? You wanna start at the top?"

"I don't want to, but I guess I will." Jackie aimed the hose at Wally's head, rinsed him front and back, and then returned her attention to where she had started.

The Writer

"It seems that we both have goosebumps," she said playfully. "The difference is that you seem to have only one." Closing the valve on the hose, she took Wally by the hand. "We should go below."

Wally followed her into the cabin and felt his fear rising in him again. He thought for a moment that he might actually get sick. Consoling himself that it was the rocking of the boat in the waves that had made him feel that way, he fought his fear. He had told Jackie how he felt. She had told him how she felt. The barriers, artificial and totally of his own construction, had been removed. Still, however, he was nervous.

Jackie led Wally to the forward cabin. It wasn't plush, but it was nice. The cabin was located just beneath the foredeck, making the bed almost triangular in shape. Jackie turned to face Wally and sat on the edge of the bed, looking up at him.

"Are you okay with this?" she asked, demonstrating her sensitivity to Walter's problems.

Wally glanced down to where she was caressing him and said, "Parts of me are. Let's give it a try and see if the rest of me is."

Jackie smiled broadly and scooted backward onto the bed, where she leaned up against a pillow and parted her legs.

"Well, come on then." She urged him to join her.

Wally had made the right choices. He had waited. He knew what he wanted and he had waited. He was right and Kelly was wrong. Making love was the right choice. Instinctively, Wally matched his movement to the rocking of the boat. The result was that their dance was slow and rhythmic, extending both their lovemaking and their ecstasy.

229

The Writer

Nestled together in the afterglow, Wally whispered, "Thank you."

"You don't need to thank me for that. I enjoyed it too, you know," Jackie replied softly.

"I know," Wally said. "I could tell. Nobody could fake ... well ... that." Jackie's earthquake would be forever seared into his memory.

"I meant to thank you for helping me conquer my fears; for bringing me out of my comfortable, but sad, solitude." Wally squeezed her. "I was a 41 year old loser until ... recently."

Jackie stroked his face gently with her hand. "No you weren't. You were a 41 year old lost treasure. Promise me that you'll keep writing."

"I will," Wally promised. The rocking of the boat and their exhaustion led them into a deep and restful sleep. It was almost ten when Jackie stirred again.

"Wally," she whispered. "I need to pee again. Do I have to go back into the bay?"

Wally laughed. "No. There's a head just outside the cabin door."

Jackie crawled to the end of the bed.

"Read the instructions!" he called after her.

They sailed back to the dock under the moonlight.

CHAPTER TWENTY-THREE

SUNDAY MORNING

"You fucked her, didn't you?" Kelly asked.

"No." Wally defended himself. "I ... I mean *we*, made love. It was mutual. It was passionate. It was wonderful."

"When we first met, you said something about fast cars and faster women," Kelly persisted. "Well, for you, getting a girl into bed after only one month is pretty damn fast. I think you were just doing research."

"You're an ass," Wally muttered. "You're worse than an ass. You're a jealous ass. You're just mad because you didn't get to fuck Giselle, the blonde cheerleader, or the nun."

"Dumbass," Kelly sneered. "You're the one that wanted to do Giselle – and Melodie too, if I recall."

"Oh. Yeah," Wally conceded the point – then reversed himself. Sometimes it was hard to their keep carnal desires separated, even though the schizophrenic personalities were quite distinct.

"No. It was *you* who wanted Giselle. I had to talk you out of it."

"You mean *write* me out of it," Kelly shot back.

The Writer

"And I invented the nun to keep you from chasing after the hang glider. I'm pretty sure neither of us wanted to do Melodie."

"Well, I kinda did," Kelly admitted, "but Bill was there and I didn't see an opening."

Wally was on a roll. "It was you who wanted me to let you fuck the blonde cheerleader. It was you who wanted Kent Clarkson to fuck Lucy!"

"You're the one who dreamed about the naked cheerleader doing you in a life raft," Kelly parried at least one of the charges leveled by Wally.

The two men stared at each other, neither blinking for at least ten seconds. Wally was just about ready to erase Kelly Blanton from the tablet, when Kelly broke down.

"Whoa!" Kelly reined Wally in. "You do realize that this is the poster child for circular arguments. After all, I'm your alter-ego, not a different person."

Wally agreed and calmed down. All of Kelly's lust resided in Wally too; it was just repressed.

Kelly tried to explain himself.

"Let's just say that I'm trying to make sure that you didn't fuck Jackie. I'm trying to make sure that you made love to her. I'm challenging you just to make sure that you're sure."

"Oh, man?" Wally whined. "I don't know. I've never even been close to being in love. I never had feelings for a woman." Wally's insecurities were returning.

"No, man," Kelly cautioned. "Don't regress. Just don't do anything stupid."

The Writer

"Okay," Wally agreed. "I hear ya."

"Listen. As long as we're talking, I've been reading some of our work and those coincidences I mentioned before are really starting to bother me." Kelly turned on the tablet.

"What do you mean?" Wally asked.

"Look here." Kelly took Wally on a tour. "You wrote a summary for *Twisted* about a shipwreck. The next day we came across a sailboat that had run aground. You wrote about the dive trip – the one with six women. The next day, we had six women on the boat with us. What are the odds? The most striking one was *Hang it All*. You wrote almost exactly what happened only a few hours later."

Kelly had captured Walter's imagination if not his concurrence. Walter thought that there might be a good story line in there somewhere, so he pressed Kelly for details.

"What about that series with Brandon, the cowboy and the lady in the Cadillac? None of that came true, did it? Did you read about a rape or kidnapping on the highway?"

"I can't read a paper by myself, dumbass," Kelly sneered. "There was also the story about the dirigible, and the kids playing the party version of baseball. Oh, and the race car driver."

"You make a good point about not being able to read the paper – at least not without me knowing about it." Wally picked up the tablet. "Let's see what Mr. Google has to say, shall we? I'm going to prove to you that this is nothing more than coincidence, contrived coincidence."

Not long afterwards, Wally was cursing. Searching the news reports, Walter had learned that a woman had been kidnapped,

The Writer

raped and murdered on a highway on the other side of the state. The kidnapper had also killed a man and a woman bystander. In another story, the wife of a jockey had tried to kill him. That one turned out differently though. When she confronted her husband, he happened to be with his mistress. A stable hand had followed his girlfriend, the mistress, to the jockey's home and had burst in on them as well. It was the stable hand who ended up killing the mistress and the jockey.

"Coincidence." Wally stuck to his guns. "What about Eddie? Where's his story? In fact, have you figured out how he got in the ice yet?"

"No," Kelly admitted, "but that's beside the point. You didn't write that one. I did."

"Coincidence." Wally wouldn't budge.

"Okay, Mr. *Doubting Thomas*," Kelly persisted. "I didn't want to go this far, but look at *Walter Finds a Woman*."

"What about it?" Wally was in denial.

"You wrote about meeting a hot chick in a grocery store. You actually meet a hot chick in a bookstore. You wrote about a nice dinner. You had a nice dinner. You wrote that the woman wanted to see you again. Jackie said the same thing. If she hadn't, you'd have collected your writer's guide and never gone back."

Wally was catching on.

"I wrote that Tatum and I dated. Jackie and I dated. I wrote that I fell in love with Tatum. I fell in love with Jackie. I wrote that it would be alright to make love if I was *in* love. Right after I admitted that I was in love with Jackie, we made love." Wally's mind was

234

The Writer

swirling. He looked at Kelly. "I wrote that I met Tatum and fell in love with Miss Tait. Is that a coincidence?"

Kelly shrugged.

"I wrote that I proposed to Tatum and we got engaged. But that was all just fantasy!" Wally returned to his state of denial. He thought furiously. "Okay. Why is the story about Tatum so close to what really happened and the other stories are full of inconsistencies. What happened to the blonde cheerleader?"

"You forgot to save that story, remember? Instead, you met Giselle. You met someone, but not the one you described in the story," Kelly said. "You erased the baseball game. You erased the dirigible accident. Whatever you type and save seems to come true. The similarities in the stories are getting stronger because you're becoming a better writer."

"This is so *Twilight Zone*," Wally muttered, remembering the old television show. "We need to test this."

"No." Kelly rejected his statement outright. "*YOU* need to test it. Whatever I write stays on the page – or in byte-world or however that thing stores what I type. But you're right. A test is in order. You need to write something and see if it comes true."

"What?" Wally wondered.

"You could have Tatum give you a blow-job and see what happens." Kelly laughed.

"No," Wally said, not even realizing what he was saying. "It has to be something that isn't likely to happen anyway." Snapping out of the distraction of making up a story, he realized what Kelly had suggested and shouted, "Screw you, Kelly! This is serious!"

The Writer

"I've got it." Wally found the story about him and Tatum. "I don't need to write a new story. I'll just add to the one that seems to have most things in common with reality now."

Wally went to the last entry about Tatum. He quickly summarized the events of yesterday, added the details to the previously sketchy outline – just to make the stories match better – and added the next events. These would be the test.

Walter Fleegle's life was coming together. He had found the woman of his dreams. He was still a failure in his new career, that of novelist, but at least one woman, Tatum, supported and encouraged him. She had given him hope. Perhaps the forces of the universe – forces known as Karma, grace, Guardian Angels, and fate – might come to a great crescendo and deliver a letter of acceptance from a publisher. Perhaps Walter was on his way to fame and fortune. He already knew what he wanted to do if that happened. He would retire from the DOT, open a small bookstore, and start a publishing company that catered to the undiscovered writer.

Walter hit save. "I'm getting lunch." He was about to ask Kelly to come along, when he realized that the emotional turmoil had taken its toll. Rather than risk indigestion, he decided to meditate first and try to regain his composure.

Seated on the floor, Walter closed his eyes. After spending ten minutes sifting through the memories of Jackie's naked body, he

The Writer

was able to begin to eliminate other distractions as well. When he got to Kelly again, he accepted the fact that he had needed Kelly in order to break out of the doldrums created by his habits, but that Kelly needed to become what he had been intended to be all along: Kelly Blanton was a pen name. He was a persona to hide behind, not one to succumb to. With that done, Wally realized that blaming Kelly for not figuring out how to put Eddie into the ice was wrong. It was not Kelly's fault.

Wally reviewed the situation. Eddie was a private detective. He was following leads trying to find a missing person. Those took him to Alaska where two opposing groups had squared off in a very emotional battle over hunting. How to get Eddie into the ice – that was the question. *Got it*. Wally thought. He typed it up.

Eddie had followed the missing girl to Alaska. She was on a crazy mission to document the environmental conflict between the hunters and the activists. It wasn't hard to find her. She wasn't a professional and didn't spend a lot of time looking over her shoulder. When Eddie did catch up to her, she had her camera set up on an ice floe taking pictures of one of the hunters. Since one group of hunters was hunting polar bears and the other was hunting the hunters, she had no friends at all – none except Eddie. Eddie had heard the gunfire from his rubber power boat. He had been patrolling the coast looking for signs of his own quarry. When he rounded a small iceberg the situation became clear. The girl was filming a gun battle between the eco-

The Writer

terrorists and the bear hunters. Whichever group won, would probably shoot her next. Eddie ran his rubber boat up onto the ice and grabbed her, tossing her into the boat. He shoved it off of the ice again and began to climb in. A bullet grazed his head and he fell. Because he was wearing a full, cold-weather protective suit, which included a very hard piece of headgear, like a construction worker's hat on steroids, the bullet knocked him out, but didn't penetrate. When he fell, he slid into the water. The girl was terrified and after watching him float motionless for a minute, put the outboard into gear and left. Over the next few hours, the current kept Eddie next to the ice and the water froze around him. Snow drifted over the top of where he floated, making an air pocket. When the snow and ice eventually froze together, Eddie was entombed.

Walter saved the file and went to get his lunch. He'd earned it.

The Writer

CHAPTER TWENTY-FOUR

ACCEPTANCE

Walter didn't want to do it. He was afraid – again. It was Sunday afternoon and everything seemed to be going pretty well. He'd admitted to himself and to Jackie that he was in love. He'd finished the story line for *Ice* and could start to add detailed text. He figured that he could flesh out the story in a month if he worked on it every night. He'd gotten Kelly under control. He'd resolved his flirtation with schizophrenia. But he was still afraid. He'd just had a good lunch and didn't want to lose it. Wally stared at his tablet. He had mail. It was from a publisher – Ranger Books.

Swallowing hard, he opened the email. Slowly a grin appeared, then a smile, and then he exploded into joyous laughter.

Dear Mr. Blanton,

We at Ranger Books are pleased to inform you that your query has been well received by our review team. The only uncertainty is how your main character became entrapped in the ice. If that part is not credible, then the story will be weak. But if you can send a synopsis that satisfies our team, we will begin contract negotiations immediately.

The Writer

Thank you for your query. We look forward to
hearing from you soon.

Walter danced and bounced around the apartment for ten
minutes before he could calm down enough to call Jackie.

"Hello?" she answered.

"I'm in! I'm in! I got an acceptance letter!" he babbled.
"There's a condition, but the odd thing is that I had just ... well,
never mind. It's an odd coincidence. I'll tell you all about it. I want
to have a celebration! I want to celebrate with you!"

Thirty minutes later, Walter Fleegle pulled up to Jackie's
apartment. She rushed outside to greet him, throwing her arms
around his neck, and hugging him for all she was worth. She
straddled the bike behind him and snuggled up close. Wally drove
to a local bar – it was more of a pub, really – and they went inside to
celebrate. Wally had been to the pub before. Finnegan's was a nice
place. It was quiet, not like the sports bars that seemed to be in
abundance. Finnegan's was a place to drink and talk – except on
St. Patrick's Day, of course.

Wally and Jackie entered like a king with his queen. Wally
pointed at Mick behind the bar and ordered a bottle of Tullamore
Dew for the happy couple and a round for everyone in the house.
Both of the other patrons laughed. It was Sunday afternoon and
they were in the only bar in town without a television set.

"Okay!" Walter was not to be deterred. "Two rounds!"

Jackie and Walter spent the next two hours sitting in
Finnegan's, sipping whiskey, and getting to know each other better.

The Writer

At the end of the evening, both Mick and Jackie insisted that they get a cab. They could come back for the bike in the morning.

Jackie also insisted that Wally stay the night at her apartment. Wally would recall the next morning that his first impression of her place was that it had smelled good. It did occur to him that they'd been on several dates and that this was the first time he had come inside. He didn't care. He was still elated. Jackie guided him to the bedroom where they celebrated for another 40 minutes before drifting off to sleep.

In the morning, still riding high, they showered – together of course – celebrated again and then called a cab to take Walter to his place. Walter would have to get his bike later. As it was, he would only just make it to work on time.

In the toll booth office, Walter shared the news with Jack. Of course, Jack had been the one that got him started on his new life and Wally told him that he would dedicate the first book to him. The day seemed interminable. After he had completed his shift, he took his scooter back to his apartment, called a cab to go get his bike, and went to see Jackie again.

After they had celebrated some more and were lying in bed, cooling off and catching their breath, Jackie whispered, "I think I've created a monster! Are you going to try to catch up on all 20 years of celibacy in one week? Or do I get a rest?"

Suddenly, Walter's elation over being in love and having been accepted, both as a man and an author, turned to stark terror.

"I'm sorry!" he started sweating again, but for a new reason. "Please forgive me! I don't know how often people do this. I don't know what's normal!" He was actually starting to hyperventilate.

The Writer

"I'll tell you what. Until I get the hang of things, I will always let you be the initiator." Wally's face was screaming for forgiveness.

Jackie smiled and comforted him.

"Okay. But only for a while. I like it when I see that you want me. I like it when you are the one to … get frisky."

The Writer

CHAPTER TWENTY-FIVE

RETIREMENT

Two months later, Jackie and Walter rode up to the toll booth on Walter's Triumph and went inside. Walter was retiring early. Jack and a few of the other attendants were throwing him a little party. It didn't matter to Walter, Jack, or any one of the others, that it was a small party. Toll collectors spend most of their lives alone amongst the masses. They see thousands of people every day, some each and every day as they commute, but they hardly ever have the time to get to know any of them.

After the brief ceremony, Jack asked Walter for a short speech. It was supposed to be a way to embarrass and intimidate the retiree, but it backfired. Walter thanked Jack for everything. He thanked his co-workers for being friends and then he made his announcement.

"As you know, my manuscript has been accepted and my first book is coming out in about four months. I say my first, because I've got enough characters collected on the tablet that Jack gave me to write a hundred books." Everyone applauded.

"What you don't know is that I've been lucky enough to get struck by Lady Luck's lightning twice." Walter took Jackie's hand. "I'd like you all to meet the future Mrs. Walter Fleegle."

Everyone applauded again and then went back to work.

The Writer

Walter and Jackie spent almost every evening and night together for the next three months. They still celebrated Walter's success frequently, but Jackie was getting her rest. Walter's retirement was looking very promising indeed. On more than one occasion, he had thought that h s retirement was going to be better than his working life had been. That part wasn't a new concept – it was the *why* it was going to be better that made Wally so happy.

Jackie still spent most of her days working at home and Wally spent most of his days working from his apartment. There were edits sent to him by Ranger Books that he had to consider. Accepting or rejecting them one at a time took days. He had to retype stiff paragraphs, write promotional pieces, and approve things: cover designs, facebook designs, webpage designs, and audio trailers for radio advertising. He hadn't been offered an advance, but his retirement pay from the DOT was more than sufficient for his still minimal needs.

In the evening, when Wally would go to Jackie's place, he often brought his tablet with him. After dinner and before bed, Jackie would sit and read while Wally would sit and write. Neither of them watched much television.

Unlike a lot of engaged couples, Wally and Jackie did not spend hours and hours worrying about the *who, what, where, and when* of their wedding. Their plans revolved around Wally's first royalty check. Both of them were frugal and knew that marriage meant a merging of property and finances. Both of them wanted to make sure that there would be ro problems.

The Writer

CHAPTER TWENTY-SIX

A GOOD USE FOR A MAN

Life for Walter and Jackie had become comfortable and close. Another month had passed and Ranger Books was starting to hint at a publication date. That meant that a royalty check might soon follow and that meant that they could get married.

In the meantime, life went on.

Walter Fleegle sat at a small table on the balcony of Jackie's apartment. They had just finished dinner, which Walter had prepared – Jackie wasn't much of a cook. Jackie slid open the heavy glass door, and poked her head out.

"I need to run out and get some new shoes. Do you wanna come with me?"

Wally grinned his now well-practiced crooked smile and shook his head.

"I think I'll stay here. I've got some ideas for the plot line of the next book and need to get them typed up."

Jackie smiled broadly.

"The next one?" she bubbled. "So, you're really going to make this work, huh?"

"I hope so!" Wally laughed. "No promises!"

The Writer

Jackie slid the door closed and, shortly afterwards, Walter heard her go out. It was time for him to get to work. Stretching, as he often did after a good meal, Wally extracted himself from the pleasant comfort of the porch and went inside. The tablet was on the coffee table, so he plopped onto the couch and picked it up. He'd often thought it to be an interesting conjunction of fate that he and Jackie had the exact same tablet in the exact same color. He'd even used that to make points in his argument with Kelly about coincidences.

He picked it up and tapped the screen.

The expression on Walter Fleegle's face changed from mild surprise to intense curiosity as the screen came to life. This wasn't his tablet; it was Jackie's.

Jackie had apparently left her tablet turned on, but more than that, she had left a file open. The layout was very familiar to Wally. It seemed as though Jackie was writing her own book. The main text took up the greater part of the screen, and along the left side, there was a column that looked like a table of contents. It was the text on the screen, however, that had riveted Wally's attention to the tablet and froze his soul.

Walter's manuscript is nearly through the editing process, Jackie thought to herself. That meant that they could be married in a few more months. She cursed herself for procrastinating so long. Everything had been going so well that she kept putting off deciding how she would kill him. Murder takes intense, detailed, and intricate planning. Jackie needed to get started.

The Writer

What the fuck is this? Walter thought. He scanned the table of contents. At the top was what appeared to be the title of the book: *A Good Use for a Man.*

The list of Chapter titles included:

Finding the Right Man

The Day I Met William

Make Him Love Me

Baiting the Trap

Knitting the Cocoon

Finding Freedom

Walter Fleegle's mind swirled through various states of confusion, intertwined with intense emotional explosions. *Who's William?* He asked. *If this is about a guy named William, why is Walter mentioned in the text?*

Wally tapped the screen, selecting the chapter about finding the right man. He read what she had written and the emotions inside him reached hurricane strength. Jackie's editing job wasn't editing at all — at least in her book. Jackie-in-the-book is a beta-reader. She's a screener: a sieve for an agent at a publishing house. Jackie-in-the-book reads one or two books a week that have been submitted to her boss by aspiring writers — just like Wally. If she likes one of them, she gives the agent a positive recommendation. In the chapter on *Finding the Right Man*, Jackie-in-the-book selects

The Writer

a writer using very simple criteria. He has to be very good and he has to be single. Walter couldn't help notice that he fit the criteria.

The next chapter, *The Day I Met William,* calmed Wally slightly. William was not Walter. He was handsome, tall, and charismatic. According to the story, Jackie-in-the-book met William at an Art Museum. All that seemed to put distance between Wally and her story – except for that part about the museum. When Jackie wrote about how Jackie-in-the-book followed William for two weeks before manufacturing what would seem to be a chance encounter, Wally started to spiral into disorientation once again.

The chapter titled *Make Him Love Me* was filled with flirting, sexual innuendo, and eventually sexual encounters, but it was also filled with how Jackie-in-the-book encouraged William, urging him to complete his manuscript and get it submitted to a publisher.

It was in the chapter *Baiting the Trap* that William disappeared from the text and Walter's name occurred for the first time. Walter read one paragraph six or seven times to make sure he had read it correctly.

Jackie's plan was going well. She had found her writer and made him fall in love with her. Strangely, it had been harder to do than she had anticipated; she'd had to resort to flaunting her sexuality, numerous subtle sexual references, and blatant ego stroking. Jackie, however, was determined and eventually, Wally had proclaimed his love. Now it was time for Jackie to make her move. She very carefully prepared an email to the agent she worked

The Writer

for and strongly recommended a new novel titled *Ice*,
by Kelly Blanton.

Walter almost threw up. Jackie's agent worked for Ranger Books. Walter tapped the next chapter: *Knitting the Cocoon*.

Through a combination of tears and anger, Walter Fleegle read about how Jackie-in-the-book intended to conclude their relationship. When Kelly received his first royalty check, Jackie-in-the-book would be assured that he would be successful as an author: financially successful. She would marry Wally, creating joint property. She would own half of the rights to their novel. After adding a little life insurance that Jackie-in-the-book made sure would cover lost future income, she calculated his net potential worth and concluded the chapter with a commitment to find her freedom: freedom born of Walter's death and a big payout.

Weakened by the emotional energy he had expended, Wally tapped the last chapter. In *Finding Freedom*, Jackie-in-the-book had come down with writer's block. It was that chapter that had been open when Wally inadvertently picked up Jackie's tablet and discovered her novel.

He was about to put the tablet down, when Kelly said, "This could all be coincidence. Why don't you check the meta-data and see when Jackie wrote these things?"

It was good advice: good advice with a horrifying outcome. The dates listed for when each chapter had been created and last edited proved that Jackie had begun writing her story well before meeting Wally. One date, the one about reading *Ice*, jived with when the query had been sent. In a fit of near insanity, Walter

The Writer

accessed Jackie's email and found her recommendation to Ranger Books.

Wally closed the email account and pulled up the place in Jackie's book that had been on the screen when he picked it up. Pushing the button to put the tablet to sleep, Wally replaced the device on the coffee table in exactly the same place that it had been before he had picked it up.

Glancing at his watch, he realized that Jackie would be coming home soon. He was a mess. He didn't know what to do but he knew that he had to get control. Wally got in the shower. It would calm him and cleanse him. He was still there when Jackie came home. He heard her come in, but was still uncertain about how he would handle things. He was still unsure when Jackie pulled the shower curtain back and joined him. Walter looked at her splendid body, her emerald green eyes, and welcoming smile, and saw pure evil. When she knelt down, he was at a decision point. One part of him wanted to let her finish what she'd started, but his stomach couldn't handle it. Ad-libbing instead of playing the part that she had written for him, he put his hand on her head. "I really don't feel well. Can we do this later?"

Jackie looked up at him and smiled. "Of course. But what's wrong?" She stood up and looked at Wally with what appeared to be genuine concern. Walter granted that the concern was genuine. After all, he couldn't get sick and die too soon or it would ruin her plan.

"I think I need to go home," Wally said, turning off the water and grabbing a towel. "I really don't feel well. It's in my stomach."

The Writer

Over Jackie's mild objections and offers to nurse him, Walter got dressed and left, making certain to pick up his tablet from the dining room table and not the one on the coffee table.

The Writer

CHAPTER TWENTY-SEVEN

RESOLUTION

Walter slept fitfully. His dreams swirled like a school of fish in a feeding frenzy. Tatum, William, Jackie-in-the-book, naked cheerleaders, a cowboy, a blonde girl in a Volkswagen, and a hang gliding nun came and went like special effects created for a Halloween spook house.

At 2AM, Wally woke up in a cold sweat. As he had done before, he attempted to resolve his emotions with his writing. He was desperate. While he was at Jackie's earlier – when he found her story – the mail had arrived. In it was an advance from Ranger Books. The agent Jackie worked for must be pretty good because the check was to compensate him for the pre-orders that had been received. Jackie would find out about it soon enough and it would be time for her to finalize her plans. He could stall by putting off getting married, but such a sudden change in direction on his part would lead to very unpredictable results. Recently judges had decided that people didn't even need to be married to create community property. She had encouraged him. That might be enough.

Wally started to type.

Tatum ...

252

The Writer

He stopped. Tatum didn't plot to kill Wally. How could adding to his story deflect Jackie's intentions? Maybe he needed to go back to her place and somehow edit Jackie's story? Wally rejected the idea. She'd see it.

Wally began again.

> Walter Fleegle was dead. Jackie had killed him, taken all his money, and began to live the high life. Her downfall was as dramatic and sad as her rise to the top had been. Within two months, she had become an alcoholic, slept with a different man almost every night, and had been diagnosed with three different sexually transmitted diseases. One of which, always resulted in sterility. Another one slowly ate away the nervous system, resulting in a slow, painful, and unavoidable death.

"Kinda vengeful, isn't it?" Kelly interjected.

Walter nodded through his tears and deleted the entry.

> Walter and Tatum were getting married. Everything was set. Their life together was destined to be perfect. The only hiccup in the arrangements had been on the day before they had gone to get the marriage license. Tatum had confessed that "Tatum" was not her real name. It was a nickname that she had

The Writer

acquired in college. Her real name was Jacqueline
Tait. Walter took all this in stride and the wedding
plans proceeded.

One Saturday afternoon, only a week before the
ceremony, everything changed. Walter had gone to
get fitted for his tuxedo. Jackie was home alone when
the door to her apartment exploded inward. The
creature before her was so vile and evil that it would
be hard to describe him as a man. The thing rushed at
Jackie, catching her just before she got to the door to
the balcony. He pulled her back and into the
bedroom, where he slapped her repeatedly. Virtually
tearing her clothes off of her, he violated her. Jackie
tried to deal with it calmly, accepting it, telling herself
that it would be over soon. Fate, however, had other
ideas. Her rapist's knife slide effortlessly through the
skin, muscle, and sinew of her neck, exposing her
severed arteries and wind pipe. Jackie trembled,
gurgled, and died before her attacker removed
himself.

"You think that's any better than three STDs and a slow
death?" Kelly asked. "Come on, Wally. You're better than that."

Walter deleted the passage. Kelly was right. He just wanted to
survive.

"You know this is all your fault, don't you?" Kelly asked.

254

The Writer

Wally looked at Kelly with complete disbelief. Walter's entire world had been turned inside out and Kelly was playing the guilt card.

"Yeah," Kelly answered Wally's unasked question. "You invented Tatum and Jackie invented William at about the same time. I think that Karma connected you two through your identical tablets. You're her William and she's your Tatum. William? Wally? Jackie Tait? Tatum?"

Wally continued to look dumbfounded. It was Kelly who put it together.

"Jackie didn't care who her victim was as long as he could eventually be rich. Her plan was a little different than the standard gold digger plan. She would get her man before he got rich. That way she avoided prenuptials and lots of other questions."

Finding his tongue, Wally asked, "You mean questions like why a hot chick would marry a guy like me?"

"No," Kelly said truthfully. "You're not a guy like you anymore. You're a guy like me." Kelly waited for a reaction, but getting none, he continued. "You described Tatum's body pretty well, but you know what you didn't do?"

Wally shook his head.

"You didn't give her a personality. You didn't give her character or morals." Kelly pointed at Wally and shook his finger. "It's all your fault."

"You're back on that 'write it and it comes true' kick, aren't you?" Wally shook his head again. "You're full of shit."

255

The Writer

"Maybe so. Maybe not. But if you can write your way out of this, why not give it a try?" Kelly suggested.

Wally nodded. There would be no harm.

Walter Fleegle learned that Tatum was just a nickname. Tatum's real name was Jacqueline 'Jackie' Tait. It didn't make much difference. Walter was losing interest in Tatum anyway. Walter had grown a lot in the last few months and Tatum, now Jackie, just didn't fit well anymore. Wally's problem was how to break it off without doing too much damage.

Part of what had caused Walter to question his relationship with Tatum-Jackie was a series of little clues that made Wally think that Jackie was only interested in him for financial stability.

"Oh, I like that," Kelly interrupted.

Wally ignored him.

Walter wasn't sure how to deal with it. In fact he was at a total loss. He'd made commitments to Tatum-Jackie and he wasn't the kind of man to just walk away. No, Walter thought, Tatum-Jackie needed to leave him. Being a jerk wouldn't work. If Jackie didn't care about anything but his bank account, being a jerk wouldn't drive her away. If her motivation to

The Writer

be with him was money, her motivation to leave had
to be more money.

Walter Fleegle smiled broadly, almost laughing, and continued
typing.

The next day, Tatum-Jackie came over to see
Wally. She informed him that she had won the lottery
and somehow everything seemed different. She was
different. He was different. Their relationship was
different. She was very sorry, but she wouldn't be
able to marry him.

"Do you really think this is gonna work?" Wally asked feebly.

"I'm not sure," Kelly said, but at least we can get some sleep.

"Well I can tell you one thing," Wally said. "I still don't believe
in your mystical theories. If all this isn't simple coincidence, then I
prefer to believe that my guardian angels have been at work. They
encouraged me to believe that what I wrote could actually happen,
leading me to believe in the credibility of my stories. Then they led
me to Jackie's tablet and saved me. Of course, writing these stories
also served to set goals for myself. I wanted a woman. I created a
woman. That was a goal, not a prediction. And, as you said, my
creation was incomplete. She was flawed."

Kelly started to object, but Wally stopped him.

The Writer

"Nevertheless! I'm through writing. Everything from now on will be attributed to Kelly Blanton." Wally laughed. "There's no sense in taking chances."

With that decided, Walter Fleegle was able to sleep well for the remainder of the night. In the morning, he dodged a call from Jackie and went to see if he could get his old job back at the toll booth. Kelly could write at night and Wally could spend the day in the one place where he had always felt safe.

Later that afternoon, Walter was cornered. He'd dodged two calls from Jackie during the day. He was not going to be able to avoid her any longer. She was outside his apartment. When he saw her get out of the cab, he figured that she was worried about him – for whatever reason, good or bad. Steeling himself to pretend that he was just sick, he put on a sad face and opened the door.

"Wally?" Jackie said. "I've got horrible news."

This was not what Walter had expected. He coughed slightly for effect and asked, "What's that, honey?"

"After you left last night, I got a call from an attorney in Ottawa. It seems that an uncle that I didn't even know I had has died. Apparently, I'm in his will and I have to go up there for the reading."

Wally was expecting her to ask him to go with him. Murder in Canada might be easier to get away with than murder in the States.

"Hey, dumbass," Kelly interrupted. "Yesterday she didn't even have a plan. There's no way she could have concocted a plan and made the arrangements already."

"What if she was up at two o'clock like we were?" Wally parried Kelly's logic.

258

The Writer

"That's so sad," Wally said to Jackie, adding another little cough.

"I'll see you when I get back," Jackie said, leaning in and giving him a light kiss on the cheek.

Wally closed the door. "That was not what I expected at all," he said to Kelly. Dropping into his understuffed chair, he clicked the television on to watch the news.

The crawler at the bottom of the screen proclaimed that Canadian billionaire, Hans Friedhoff, had died childless, naming a local girl, a distant niece named Jacqueline Tait, as his sole heir.

Walter Fleegle smiled. He knew that he'd never see Jackie again.

"Told ya so," Kelly teased.

"You're full of shit," Wally said still smiling.

EPILOGUE

There are writers and there are characters.

CPSIA information can be obtained
at www.ICGtesting.com
Printed in the USA
LVHW090735090119
603206LV00001B/29/P